A Twist
in the Tail

BOOKS BY LEIGHANN DOBBS

OYSTER COVE GUESTHOUSE (COZY CAT MYSTERY SERIES)

A Twist in the Tail
A Whisker in the Dark
A Purrfect Alibi

MYSTIC NOTCH (COZY CAT MYSTERY SERIES)

Ghostly Paws
A Spirited Tail
A Mew to a Kill
Paws and Effect
Probable Paws
A Whisker of a Doubt

BLACKMOORE SISTERS (COZY MYSTERY SERIES)

Dead Wrong
Dead & Buried
Dead Tide
Buried Secrets
Deadly Intentions
A Grave Mistake
Spell Found
Fatal Fortune

LEXY BAKER (COZY MYSTERY SERIES)

Lexy Baker Cozy Mystery Series Boxed Set Vol. 1
(Books 1–4)

Or buy the books separately:
Killer Cupcakes
Dying for Danish

LEIGHANN DOBBS

A Twist in the Tail

GRAND CENTRAL
PUBLISHING

NEW YORK   BOSTON

Copyright © 2019 by Leighann Dobbs
Cover design: Debbie Clement. Cover Images: Shutterstock.
Cover copyright © 2020 by Hachette Book Group, Inc.

Grand Central Publishing
Hachette Book Group
1290 Avenue of the Americas, New York, NY 10104
grandcentralpublishing.com
twitter.com/grandcentralpub

First published in 2019 by Bookouture, an imprint of StoryFire Ltd.

First Grand Central Publishing edition: July 2020

Grand Central Publishing is a division of Hachette Book Group, Inc.
The Grand Central Publishing name and logo is a
trademark of Hachette Book Group, Inc.

The publisher is not responsible for websites (or their content)
that are not owned by the publisher.

The Hachette Speakers Bureau provides a wide range of authors for speaking events. To find out more, go to www.hachettespeakersbureau.com or call (866) 376-6591.

ISBN: 978-1-5387-3620-3 (mass market)

Printed in the United States of America

OPM

10 9 8 7 6 5 4 3 2 1

A Twist
in the Tail

Chapter One

I should have known by the unsettling tone of the cats' meows that disaster was looming. Of course, at the time I was more worried about how the guests liked breakfast. It was only the fourth one I'd served since officially becoming owner of the Oyster Cove Guesthouse.

They seemed to be enjoying it. Now, don't get me wrong, it was nothing fancy. Bacon, scrambled eggs, sausage, and lemon–poppy seed muffins were the extent of my culinary expertise. Quite frankly, I might have misjudged whether my cooking skills were up to par when entering into this agreement. Maybe I should have read the fine print in the documents I'd received from Millie Sullivan, the elderly former owner.

Even though the breakfasts weren't five-star cuisine, I hadn't had any complaints from my first batch of guests. Well, all except one. Charles Prescott. He was the reason I was now hovering in the doorway holding an antique egg cup with a perfectly warm soft-boiled egg nestled inside.

Charles had complained about his egg yesterday. It was too cold. He was quite loud about it, too. Since I aimed to please, this morning I had perfectly timed the egg for his pre-announced 8 a.m. arrival in the dining room. It was now 8:05 ... Where was Charles?

My eyes scanned the room just in case I'd missed

him. But my guest count totaled five, including Charles, and four were seated and already digging into their breakfast. It was easy to tell who was there and who was not, even in such an enormous room.

Several small dining tables with white linen table-cloths sat atop a massive moss-green-and-gold oriental rug. Curtains in a complementary green-and-gold silk framed the ten-foot-tall windows that offered a bird's-eye view of the sparkling Atlantic Ocean and craggy rocks of Oyster Cove. It was summer in Maine, and Flora—who I was coming to realize was the world's worst maid—had opened one window. A soft breeze fluttered the drapes and carried in the salty scent of the ocean and the cry of gulls in the distance...or was that the cats?

Ron and Iona Weatherby sat at a small table located by the window. The adorable elderly couple had binoculars dangling from their necks and cameras at their sides. Ron was slathering a muffin with butter while Iona picked daintily at the fluffy scrambled eggs. They were a delightful couple who had come here for birdwatching and photography. Perfect guests with no complaints.

Near the buffet, Ava Grantham sat alone at a table for four. Ava was in her mid-sixties. A society colum-nist, she was a thin, bird-like woman who noticed everything that went on. She was pleasant enough to talk to and told me she'd been vacationing in Oyster Cove since she was a child, even staying at the Oyster Cove Guesthouse a few times when Millie owned it. Her plate was loaded with scrambled eggs, bacon, and sausages. I wondered how she stayed so thin.

Over by the door was the fourth guest, Tina Reeves.

She was younger than the others, probably in her mid-thirties, a bubbly blonde with wide blue eyes. She'd said she'd come to visit relatives, but I had suspicions that she had another agenda, of what I just wasn't exactly sure. Nor did it matter. As long as a guest paid the bill, I didn't care what they were up to. Tina had flawless skin and a figure like an hourglass, and no wonder. She only had about a tablespoon of scrambled eggs and three blueberries on her plate.

Still no sign of Charles. I was just deciding what to do about the rapidly cooling egg in my hand when I heard the front door open. Maybe Charles had gone out for a walk before breakfast. I backed up and stuck my head into the hallway.

Darn! It wasn't Charles. It was Barbara Littlefield, the town building inspector, and the last person I wanted to deal with right now. She'd been a thorn in my side ever since I started renovations on the old mansion. Nothing I did pleased her, and she'd already fined me for two violations that a nicer person would have overlooked. It was too late to duck back into the dining room. She'd already spotted me and was marching down the hall toward me, a sour look on her face. I stepped into the hallway to head her off so she didn't disrupt the guests' breakfasts.

"Barbara, how lovely to see you," I lied.

Barbara's scowl deepened. "I just came to double-check the permit for the gazebo outside and I noticed—"

Merow!

Barbara jerked her head toward the dining room. "Do you have cats in the dining room?"

I stepped aside to let her see in. "Of course not."

"Good, because that would be a health-code violation."

Merooo!

Was it my imagination or were the cats' cries getting louder and more insistent?

Barbara frowned down the hallway, where it sounded like the cats' latest cry had come from. "Wait a minute. That sounded like it was coming from the kitchen. That's even worse!"

Barbara stormed down the hall. I hurried after her, still balancing the egg cup in my hand. Some things are more important than Charles Prescott and his breakfast—like making sure the board of health didn't shut me down for having animals in the kitchen.

"It's not coming from the kitchen." At least, I hoped it wasn't. It actually *was* coming from that direction, but I was pretty sure it was from the west wing of the mansion, which had been closed off for extensive renovations. Not that the cats didn't hang around in the kitchen—they did. I just hoped they weren't in there right now.

"I think you're right." Barbara stopped and frowned at me. "I thought I made it clear that that decrepit wing was supposed to be closed down so no one could get in there."

See what I mean? I just couldn't win with this woman. You'd think she'd be happy the cats weren't in the kitchen, but no, she'd found something else to complain about.

"It *is* blocked off. To people. Cats are sneaky and can get into anything." Couldn't they? I wasn't exactly sure. I'd only owned the guesthouse, and thus the cats, for a short time, and had no idea what those furry little monsters could get up to. They'd been fairly well behaved so far, but the way they stared at me—with their luminous, intelligent eyes—always made me feel like they were up to something behind my back. I didn't have much experience with cats, but Millie had assured me they made great companions. Thus far, I'd been too busy learning the ropes of running the guesthouse to spend time getting to know them.

Feelings of guilt crept in. I had promised Millie I would take good care of the cats, but judging by the sounds of their meows, they were in some sort of distress. I hoped one of them hadn't found its way into the closed-off wing and been hurt. It was a mess in there, and not safe.

Mee-yow!

We continued down the hall. It felt like it was taking a long time to traverse, but that was because it really was quite long. The place *was* a mansion after all. Gigantic. It had been built by shipping magnate Jedediah Biddeford 300 years ago. I'd bought it from Millie Sullivan—my mother's best friend—whose family had owned it for the last 125 years. Judging by the looks of the west wing, that was the last time that section of the house had been updated, too. Don't even get me started on the condition of the caretakers' cottage and carriage house.

The cats were really starting to howl now, and I was getting worried. Barbara surged ahead of me, then stopped at the doorway to the west wing and turned to scowl at me.

"I thought you said this was blocked off." She gestured toward the door, which was cracked open. I swore I'd locked it shut several days ago.

The large black-and-white tuxedo cat, Nero, stood in the doorway looking up at me with his striking green eyes, as if to ask, "What took you so long?" The tortie, Marlowe, rubbed her face on my ankle. At least they weren't hurt, even though the thought of hurting them myself for causing all this trouble did briefly cross my mind.

"I don't know how this got open. Maybe the handyman?" The handyman was Millie's nephew, Mike Sullivan. I'd known he was bad news since fifth grade and would never have engaged his services, but Millie had hired him to fix up some things before I'd bought the guesthouse. The work was already paid for and I couldn't afford to turn that down. I couldn't wait to get rid of him, though. "He's probably working in here. I'll check."

"Nice try, but this still violates code four hundred and one of the state statute." Barbara whipped out her notebook, presumably to write up a violation.

Great. This was just what I didn't need. And to top it off, the stupid soft-boiled egg was now cold. I switched it to my left hand and reached out my right to shut the door. "Maybe you could overlook it just this once? It wasn't open that long and—"

Nero let out a wail and launched himself at the door before I could pull it shut. The door crashed open, revealing the run-down state of the west wing. Dust mites floated in the air, cobwebs hung from the chandeliers, water stains marred the walls. But that wasn't the worst part. The worst part was what lay at the bottom of the stairway. It was a body. Charles Prescott's to be exact. And he was deathly still.

worrying about my own problems when poor Charles had lost his life.

A momentary depression descended over me as I saw my plans for success evaporating right before my eyes. And not just financial success. There was much more than money at stake here. I'd spent most of my adult life in the shadow of my ex-husband, Clive Stonefield, a semi-famous chef. His parting words about how I was nothing without him still stung. I had been determined to prove him wrong.

The Oyster Cove Guesthouse was my opportunity to shine. My chance to prove that I, too, could be successful. I'd put all my money and hopes into this purchase and it *had* to work. At forty-six, I wasn't getting any younger, and this could be my last chance.

How much could a dead body hurt business? Didn't matter. I wasn't going to let this signal my defeat. I was going to consider it an opportunity to prove that I could succeed no matter what. After all, my daughter was just making her way in the world and I had to be a good role model.

The rustle of paper brought me out of my reverie. Barbara had whipped out her notebook and was flipping through it, probably trying to find the exact section of the building code that a dead body violated so she could write me up.

"He's dead. We better call the police," I said.

Barbara looked up from her notebook, her hawk-like gaze focusing on the stairway. "It's no wonder. Look at how the stairway collapsed." Her eyes narrowed, she craned her neck forward. "Looks like dry rot to me. This place is uninhabitable."

Chapter Two

I rushed over to the body. You may think most people would be put off by a body, and that the natural inclination would be to run in the opposite direction, but I'd been halfway to a promising career as a medical examiner when I'd given everything up in favor of my ex-husband's culinary career and raising our daughter, Emma. I didn't regret staying home for Emma. The marriage was another story. Apparently, my old medical training had kicked in. I wanted to see if anything could be done, even though it was evident by his pasty skin tone and blankly staring eyes that it was too late.

I felt for a pulse. Nothing. Charles was gone. At least he wouldn't care that his egg had cooled, which was a good thing because it was now rolling around the floor. I must've dropped it in my haste to get to the body.

Talk about inconvenient. Not only did I have a dilapidated mansion and no money to repair it with, two cats I barely knew how to care for and a building inspector salivating to write me up for even the most innocent of violations, I now also had a dead body on my hands.

Of course, it was inconvenient for Charles, too. A wave of sadness washed over me. Sure, the guy had been a bit of a pain, but he didn't deserve to die. I felt selfish

I glanced at the stairs. She had a point. Jagged edges of splintered wood stuck up where the treads had broken through. The entire banister lay on the floor, though half of it had fallen away before I even bought the place. The stairs hadn't been in good condition before this. Now, they were a disaster. But that was why I had this section of the house blocked off. Only a fool would try to navigate those stairs, which brought up two questions: How had Charles gotten in here? And why?

I didn't know what Jedediah Biddeford had been thinking when he built this place. It could have easily housed four families. Maybe he'd planned to raise several generations here. The place was enormous, with several staircases and two kitchens. Over the years, parts of it had fallen into disrepair.

Millie had told me her family had closed off the west wing a generation ago and she'd had a hard time keeping up with the rest of it. That's why she'd sold it at such a discount. Well, that and the fact that she wanted more time to go gallivanting around town causing trouble with my seventy-eight-year-old mother. Keeping an eye on her was the second reason I'd been compelled to move back to my hometown of Oyster Cove, the first being getting away from my ex.

At least the cats had quieted down. They were now sniffing around the room as if they were furry CSIs looking for clues. Nero was paying quite a bit of attention to the globe-shaped newel post that had rolled over into the corner. Marlowe was sitting beside him and watching.

"Well, I'll be a monkey's hiney. Is that Prescott?" Ava Grantham appeared in the doorway, her eyes riveted on the body. Darn it! I was hoping to keep this from the guests, lest they flee demanding a refund.

"Just a little accident," I trilled. "Go on back to the dining room. I'll put out more muffins."

But it was too late. The Weatherbys emerged beside Ava.

Iona gasped as she fumbled with her binoculars. "My word! What happened?"

Ron slid his arm around her and held her tight. "Don't look, dear."

I summoned my nothing's-wrong-go-on-your-way voice. "Just an accident, folks. Nothing to see here, really."

"Not a surprise either," Barbara said, pointing out the broken stairs. "Safety hazard. You people should be careful here."

Great. That was just what I needed, Barbara telling people that the guesthouse wasn't safe.

"Someone should call the police," Ron Weatherby said. Then in a lower voice, "Though in a small town like this, I wonder how effective they'll be at investigating the condition of those stairs."

"I'll do it," Barbara said, a bit too gleefully as she whipped out her phone.

"What's going on? I...Eek!" Tina had come to join the crowd. Her eyes were even bigger than usual. Her hand flew up to her mouth as she stared at Charles. The high-pitched squeak she'd emitted had the cats riveting their heads in her direction, their whiskers twitching. "Is that a dead body?"

Ron Weatherby transferred his attentions to Tina. He put a fatherly arm around her and patted her shoulder. "Now, now, young lady, this is nothing for you to see. Let the missus and I take you into the dining room and get you some tea."

"Great idea," I said. "We'll only be a minute here and then everyone can forget all about this."

Finally, the area cleared out. I closed my eyes, willing the police to hurry before anyone else happened by. No such luck.

"What's going on? I was up fixing the sink in the sand-dollar room and I—" Mike Sullivan skidded to a stop in front of the door, his eyes widening as they flicked from the body to my face. "Sunshine, what happened?"

The last person I wanted to deal with right now was Mike Sullivan. Mike and I went way back. I mean, *way* back. He'd been my brother Tommy's best friend growing up. I'd known him practically since I was in diapers, and the nickname "Sunshine" wasn't a term of endearment. It had come about because I wasn't exactly a morning person as a teenager. Mike and Tommy had teased me about my morning grumpiness by calling me Sunshine.

Not for the first time, I wished he would hurry up with the work Millie had paid him to do. I didn't like the dimple-inducing smirk on his face when he called me Sunshine, or the way it made his whiskey-brown eyes twinkle with mischief.

"One of the guests had an accident," I said.

Mike came to my side. "Are you okay?"

My heart almost melted at the tone of genuine concern in his voice until I remembered what a pain in the neck he'd been when I was younger. Especially that time when I'd heard he was going to ask me to the junior prom. Then he changed his mind and asked slutty Stella Dumont instead. Not that I really cared that much, now. That was decades ago and I'd been married and divorced since then, but the adolescent sting of rejection never goes away. Mike never married, but who knew how many "Sunshines" he'd gone through in all those years. Since he'd spent most of his time touring the world in the navy, I assumed it was plenty.

I swatted him away. "Of course I'm okay. I'm not the one who had the accident."

"Make way! Make way!" voices demanded from the hallway. They belonged to my mother and Millie, proving that just when you think things can't get any worse, they do. I should've known they'd be here. They had a police-scanner app on their cell phones and showed up at almost every crime scene, usually before the police did.

"Glory be, Josie, is this any way to treat the guests?" As soon as Millie stepped in the room, Nero and Marlowe swiveled their attention to their previous owner. They trotted over, winding around her ankles and purring as she bent down to pet them in a movement that belied her age.

Her eyes fell on the egg cup. "Oh, Grandma Tower's china egg cup. Why is this on the floor?" It was a miracle it hadn't broken. At least I still had some luck left.

"Not to mention the egg." My mother picked up

the soft-boiled egg and looked from Mike to me. "You young people sure get up to strange things."

"We weren't up to anything. I dropped the egg when I found Charles." I inclined my head toward the body.

"Oh." My mother's gaze moved to Charles's body, over which Millie was now standing. You'd think my mother and her best friend would be shocked to see a dead body, but apparently all the crime scenes they'd attended had hardened them.

"I don't think this will be good for business." Millie tore her gaze from the body and glanced back at the doorway, where Ava Grantham still stood. "You're not going to put this in the paper, are you, Ava?"

Ava made a face and waved her hand dismissively. "Of course not. I write society columns, not obituaries."

"Good. Now what we need to do is secure the area. Make sure it doesn't get contaminated," Millie said.

"And we need some gloves." My mother turned to me. "Josie do you have any gloves? Like maybe those yellow dishwashing gloves that Flora uses?"

"I, err..." I'd never seen Flora wearing yellow gloves, but that might be because she refused to do dishes.

"And paper bags," Millie added.

Before I could say anything, there was a commotion at the front door. The police were here.

"We're down here!" Millie yelled.

"Don't worry, we've secured the scene," Mom added.

Seth Chamberlain, the Oyster Cove sheriff, appeared in the doorway. I wasn't sure how he kept getting elected, because he was older than my mother and Millie, and about as effective in fighting crime. Given the way my mom and Millie had turned into elderly CSIs, maybe that was a compliment. Anyway, rumor had it that Seth was such a nice guy that people kept voting for him. Besides, there was hardly any crime in Oyster Cove.

"I don't see any prints in the dust here." Millie pointed at the dusty steps.

"And we haven't determined how the killer got in or out," Mom added.

Killer? Surely my mother was being overly dramatic.

"Killer? It's obvious the guy just fell down the stairs. They're unsafe!" Barbara crowed.

"Now, ladies, I'm perfectly capable of determining what happened here." Seth's tone was gruff, but I could tell by the way he looked at Millie that he had the hots for her and she could get away with just about anything.

Millie blushed and fussed with her curly cotton-white hairdo. "Why, we were just trying to help."

"I know. That was nice of you. Now how about everyone clear the area and give us room to work." Seth ushered us out.

I went willingly, my mind whirling with my mother's insinuation. I felt bad that Charles had died, but I had to wonder...would it be better for business if someone had killed him as opposed to him falling down unsafe stairs?

*

Nero licked his paw and washed behind his ear as he watched the humans leave. Worry and guilt gnawed at him. Death had come to the guesthouse and he hadn't noticed until it was too late.

"I hope Millie isn't too disappointed in us. But we sent out the alert as soon as we smelled death. It's not our fault Josie is slow in understanding our communications." Marlowe swished her tail, her eyes on Seth Chamberlain, who was inspecting the body.

"Indeed." Nero continued washing. He took pains to keep his fur shiny and silky. Even a cat on his sixth life liked to look good. You never knew when a sultry Siamese or a cute Cornish Rex might be favorable to his attentions. "But perhaps we could have prevented this before it happened. Murder is not good for business."

Marlowe jerked her head in Nero's direction. "Murder? But this is an accident. Look at the stairs."

"Things are not always as they seem." Even though the situation was not ideal for the Oyster Cove Guesthouse—not to mention it not being ideal for Charles Prescott—Nero wasn't about to pass up a chance to share some of his wisdom with the younger cat.

Nero had been watching over the guesthouse for decades now. He'd wandered past the aged estate one day and knew it should be his home. Millie's senior memory prevented her from realizing the cat had been there much longer than any normal cat would have lived. In those decades, he'd become very protective of the guesthouse.

Marlowe had joined more recently. Nero had to admit he had been a bit put out when Millie had brought Marlowe home as a young kit she'd found abandoned under a bush at the shopping mall about ten years ago, but over time he'd grown fond of his young protégé. Besides, he had to have someone to pass on his wisdom to. And she could be good company. Sometimes.

Marlowe's eyes widened. "You mean you've seen a clue that someone else was here?"

Nero simply nodded. Over at the body, Seth was taking care to leave things as undisturbed as possible for the medical examiner. The deputy, Johnnie Sanders, was taking pictures, and the part-timer, Sheila Watts, was taking notes. Nero was glad they hadn't noticed them and shooed them out. Cats weren't usually welcome at crime scenes, but he'd learned that he could make himself practically invisible to humans if he was quiet and slowly slunk around, low to the ground. It worked well for sneaking into rooms and buildings too, though getting out could be a challenge if the humans shut the doors on you.

"You think he came through that door up there and the stairs simply gave way?" Sheila pointed to the top of the stairs.

"Looks that way." Sheriff Chamberlain leaned closer to the broken stairway. "These treads have rotted and the banister must have fallen off."

"That might have even happened before." Sheila inspected the edges of some upper treads still intact. "There's dust here in the holes, so I think part of the banister might have fallen off long ago."

"Even more dangerous." Seth looked at the body. "What kind of fool would attempt these stairs, especially with no railing?"

Nero glanced at Marlowe. He wished the young cat would hurry up and find the clue before Seth Chamberlain made a faulty decision about the manner in which Charles Prescott met his maker. Honestly, it was too bad that humans only had one life, otherwise Charles would be walking around in no time, and they wouldn't have this problem on their hands.

"Did you notice anything unusual last night?" Nero asked. "I was chasing mice in the attic and catnapping in between courses. I didn't hear a thing." He was only into the early part of his sixth life, and certainly not anywhere near the age his hearing should be going.

Marlowe shot him a sheepish glance. "I...err...I may have gone down to the wharf."

Nero raised a brow. "You don't say?" He didn't want to get into Marlowe's nightly activities. Girls would be girls. He could already see that the cat felt guilty, and he wasn't her parent, just her mentor.

"I just hope we haven't let Millie down," Marlowe said.

"Yes, it's unfortunate this has happened so soon after she entrusted the future of the guesthouse to us," Nero said.

Marlowe hung her head. "We have failed our first important task."

"We may still be able to redeem ourselves. If we can help solve this quickly, it may not hurt things too badly. You know what short-term memories humans have. The sooner the case is closed, the sooner they will move their attentions to something else. Making sure the guesthouse survives is of utmost importance. Millie entrusted that task to us." Nero frowned. "I do wish it didn't come with that human, Josie. She isn't as savvy as Millie."

Marlowe continued sniffing the perimeter of the

room. "Yeah, but she does come in handy for doing the menial work like laundry, cleaning, and cooking. And apparently since she came with the guesthouse, we need to be as loyal to her as we were to Millie."

Nero nodded. "I agree about the loyalty part. The cooking part needs work. She's always burning things. Not like our Millie."

"As long as she fills our dishes."

Nero joined Marlowe in sniffing. "Have you picked up the scent of a stranger?"

"No. Just the usual people and those who were in here this morning. There is something spicy, but I can't quite place it. Oh, and Stella Dumont."

Nero nodded sagely. Stella Dumont owned Smugglers Bay, just over the crest of the hill. They could even see the gulls that circled her deck from the side yard. Darn nuisance those gulls were. Apparently she'd been coming around the guesthouse to see Mike. "Yes, but we already know she comes here often."

"True, but I hope it is Stella that snuck in, because that would help us immensely. She owns a rival inn, and if she was out of the way, that might mean more guests would come here."

Nero swished his tail thoughtfully. "Indeed. Perhaps Stella was thinking that a dead body marring the reputation of the Oyster Cove Guesthouse would bring more business to *her* place."

Marlowe narrowed her eyes. "Yes, she could be the culprit."

"Are you sure there *is* a culprit?" Nero asked.

"Wait, I thought you said there was."

"Maybe there is, maybe there isn't. You need to investigate."

"You mean look at the clues. The stairs. The things the police are taking pictures of."

Nero nodded. "But perhaps they are not looking at something they should be. They are investigating under the assumption that he fell down the stairs."

"Oh, right!" Marlowe was quick on the uptake. She turned her attention away from the stairs, sniffing along the edge of the wall where a pile of debris lay—railing for the stairs, wallpaper that had fallen off the wall, and a metal wall sconce. She stopped when she came to the newel post cap—a large metal ball with a point at the end.

It had been before his time, but Nero's fine senses told him that before this wing had gone to ruin, the staircase had been a focal point, with honey oak stairs and a scrolled railing that ended in the carved newel post, the gilt globe sitting atop. He could almost picture the ladies in their gowns descending to the room once filled with velvet sofas and mahogany side tables. He figured the rounded top of the newel post had been an ornamental focal point of the stairway. Last night, someone had found a more sinister use for it.

Marlowe sniffed the round cap a few times, then shot Nero a triumphant look. "There's blood on here, but the post is not near the body. Charles couldn't have hit his head on it during the fall."

Nero nodded in satisfaction. "Very good, little one. Now how do we alert the police to our findings?"

"Easy." Marlowe put her paw on the post, pushed and let out a howl.

Seth, Sheila, and Johnnie jerked their heads in Marlowe's direction as the ball rolled toward them.

"Hey, you cats, shoo! We're investigating!" Sheila made shooing motions with her hands.

"Yes, you cats shouldn't be here." Seth tried to sound menacing, but Nero knew the sheriff liked cats because sometimes he fed them donut holes from his police cruiser when no one was looking.

Nero trotted over to the ball and looked up at Seth. "Meow!"

Seth's gaze flicked from Nero to the ball. Then he squinted and craned his neck forward. Johnnie was about to pick the ball up when Seth shot out a hand to stop him. "Hold on."

Seth's knees popped as he squatted. He pulled a pair of reading glasses out of his top pocket and slid them on his nose, squinting at the ball.

"What is it?" Sheila was still shooing the cats with her hands.

Seth glanced back at the body, then at the stairs, then pointed at a dark spot on the ball. "Guess these cats do come in handy. This here looks like blood. And if I'm not mistaken, this round piece matches the indentation on the back of the victim's head. I think we've got a murder on our hands."

Chapter Three

"Murder? Why, I can't believe it!" Millie said after Seth had given us the bad news. Mom, Millie, and I had adjourned to the parlor and were settling into the over-stuffed chairs arranged around a low marble-topped table as a private seating area.

Barbara had rushed off, probably to file a complaint against me. Or maybe she was poring over the town statutes to see what kind of fine one can dole out for having a dead body in your guesthouse. Tina had taken the news of the murder very hard and the Weatherbys had taken her upstairs with Ava, after stopping in the dining room for a snack.

"It's awful." My mother looked at me. "Who do you think would have wanted him dead?"

"He's been staying here a few days. Did you notice him arguing with anyone?" Millie asked.

Just me. "Not really. He kept to himself mostly."

"Hmm…what about the other guests? Have they been acting suspiciously?"

Had they? I had been too busy trying not to burn breakfast and dealing with Barbara Littlefield to notice. "I don't think so. Quite frankly I've had my hands full. And now this, and who knows what kind of a punishment Barbara is cooking up. Do you think she can have the guesthouse shut down?"

"Why would she do that?" Millie asked.

"I don't know, it seems like she has it in for me. I try to do everything to the codes and still she persists on finding things wrong."

"Well, she is very strict about the building codes, dear, but it's for a good reason. I'm sure she doesn't have anything against you personally." My mother patted my arm. "It's all for the good of the town. She wants to maintain the quaint atmosphere."

Millie nodded. "She can be a stickler, but she's protecting us. I mean, look at the good she did with those lousewort plants."

"She was instrumental in putting a stop to that big hotel on the cliff—what do you think would've happened to the guesthouse if that had been built?" My mother glanced out the window in the direction of the shore.

I had to give Barbara that. Last summer she'd discovered growing up on the cliffs a plant, very rare in Maine, called Furbish's Lousewort. She formed a committee and petitioned the state to declare the area where it grew protected, and in the nick of time. Some big conglomerate had been finalizing plans to build a huge hotel up there.

"But why be so hard on the guesthouse? It's one of the oldest buildings in town and I fully intend to renovate it in keeping with the way it was back in the day."

"You left town, so you're sort of an outsider in Barbara's eyes. She doesn't trust you yet. Give her time."

The cats came in and trotted over to Millie without even giving me a glance. Guess they'd forgot who their owner was now. I had to admit I was a little bit jealous of the way they settled in on Millie's lap.

"I guess the cats prefer their old owner," I said, earning a cold glare from Nero.

"Owner?" Millie was aghast. "Cats don't have owners, dear, it's the other way around. The sooner you realize that, the better your relationship with them will be."

Nero shot me a smug look and then curled up and went to sleep.

"I have to say, though, I don't know what this town is coming to," my mother said. "First dead gulls then dead people."

"Now, Rose. Don't you worry," Millie said. "Why there's been hardly any problems here in town for decades. We're due, and now that we've had these two pieces of bad luck it'll be smooth sailing from here on out."

I hoped Millie was right. I had invested everything I had into the purchase of the guesthouse and was counting on it being filled with guests for the summer season. The dead seagulls weren't a problem for me, though. Gulls generally stayed away from the guesthouse, possibly because of the cats. If that was the case, I'd have to thank them. Seagulls could be annoying pests and I didn't want them swooping around and driving away business. While I didn't wish harm on any of God's creatures, I wasn't going to cry about fewer gulls. Then again, having dead birds wash up on the beach, like they had been doing lately, wasn't very attractive to tourists either.

There was a sound at the door and I turned to see Mike.

"I thought I heard you, Auntie." Mike gave Millie a peck on the cheek then turned to my mother. "Rose, how are you?"

"Just fine, Michael. Tommy said to say hi to you by the way."

Mike winked at me. My mom had been calling him Michael since childhood, no matter how many times he told her he preferred Mike. "How is Tommy doing?"

My mother rolled her eyes. "Good, except he seems to think Maine is too far to come for a visit."

My brother Tommy had moved to Florida a few years ago and now claimed Maine was too cold for him and only came to visit twice a year. I personally thought maybe he didn't come often because Mom's antics with the crime scenes and all were a bit much for him. Luckily, I was here to try to rein her in…not that that was working out very well.

Mike gave my mother a sympathetic look and turned to me. "Hey, Sunshine, I heard about the police verdict that your guest was actually murdered. I was wondering if I could do anything to help?"

"I don't think I really need any help, do I?"

Mike shrugged. "I don't know, but I'll tell you one thing, I'm almost positive someone messed with those stairs."

I frowned. "Why would someone do that?"

"To mask the murder, of course, dear," Millie said, as if I was some kind of a dunce.

My mother nodded. "Yes, of course. They were

probably hoping Sheriff Chamberlain would say that it was an accident."

Huh, that was interesting. He almost *did* say it was an accident…and hadn't Ron Weatherby mentioned that small-town police forces usually didn't have the capacity to investigate thoroughly? I hoped that wouldn't be the case here; a murder was bad enough but an unsolved one was even worse.

"What kind of tampering do you mean?" I asked Mike. If someone had murdered Charles on purpose, then tried to stage it as an accident, they would've spent a bit of time in that room. But that section had been blocked off, the doors locked. I supposed anyone could have picked the lock, and the sounds of tools echoing through the guesthouse wasn't uncommon since Mike was working on repairs.

"The stairs were pretty rotten, but it looked like someone helped them along. The way the boards broke look like they were snapped in two as opposed to breaking from the pressure of someone standing on them. And the nails had been pulled up."

I wasn't sure what to do with this information. Tell the police? Could they figure that out on their own? And what did Mike know about stairs anyway? Sure, he was doing carpentry work here, and he seemed to be doing a good job, but he'd been a navy officer before. Carpentry was just a sideline.

I was just about to open my mouth to say as much when Flora bustled in, her white orthopedic shoes squeaking as she sashayed toward Mike.

Flora was a skinny elderly woman with gigantic

round glasses that made her eyes owlish. When Millie had sold me the Oyster Cove Guesthouse she'd said that Flora had been the maid for fifty years and depended on the money. I mean, who can live on Social Security? I assumed that meant she actually did some cleaning, and since I was from out of town and didn't know of anyone else, I agreed to keep her on. The joke was on me. Since I'd been here she'd managed to wiggle out of every job I'd tasked her with. Naturally, I didn't have to keep her on, but who could fire a little old lady with thirty-two grandchildren? I didn't have the heart for it. Maybe someday, when funds allowed, I'd get another maid who actually worked.

"Mr. Mike, are you done in the sand-dollar room?" Flora blinked up at him. It was a long ways up, too, since Flora was about four feet tall and Mike was over six.

Mike smiled down at her, turning on that boyish charm that I remembered from long ago. Apparently it wasn't only reserved for young girls. Of course that kind of charm didn't work on me anymore but it worked on Flora, who practically swooned. "I am. Did I leave too much of a mess in there?"

Flora shook her head. "Oh, no. I'm happy to clean up anything you leave."

My mouth practically fell open. Since when was Flora happy to clean?

Mike bent down and gave her a little kiss on her papery cheek. "Thanks. You let me know if it's too much." He turned to me. "And you let me know if I can help out, Sunshine."

We all watched him leave, Flora's gaze on a specific

part of his body clad in faded jeans. As soon as he cleared the door, Flora turned to me, a scowl on her face.

"I hope you don't have any ideas about me cleaning up that mess in the west wing. I do not do crime scenes."

And with that she turned and left the room, brushing past Ava Grantham in the doorway.

"I've just been upstairs and Tina is finally settled down. Young people these days, they can't handle anything worth a monkey's patootie. Good thing those Weatherbys have clear heads. Your sheriff is up in Prescott's room. He'll be interviewing all of us soon." She pulled over a straight-back chair and plopped down in it. "Honestly, I'm not surprised someone murdered Prescott."

"You're not?" we asked in unison.

Ava shook her head. "Nope, not at all. He was a nasty man."

My mother and Millie exchanged a glance.

"You knew him?" Millie asked.

"Of course." Ava pointed to herself. "This old bird's been around for a while. We worked together on a few newspapers."

"Charles worked in news? Was he a writer?" I asked.

Ava gave me a funny look. "You don't know who he was?"

I didn't like the way that sounded. Was Charles someone I was supposed to know? Knowing someone who'd been murdered in my guesthouse might not be good for business . . . or my freedom.

"No idea," I said.

"Charles Prescott was the Laughing Gourmet. You know...the food critic and chef."

Darn! I probably *should* have known who he was. Hadn't Clive—my ex—mentioned his name before? The truth was, I really hadn't paid much attention to what was going on with the ex's chef job in the later years. When we were first married I'd been very involved, always eating at his restaurants and going out to events with him, but then Emma came along and we agreed my focus should be on taking care of her needs. I started paying less and less attention to what was going on with Clive, because his career was going well and he was working his way to the top of his field. Little did I know he was also working his way to the top of a succession of pretty female sous-chefs.

"I might have heard of him," I said.

"Well, I wouldn't be surprised if you hadn't. Truth is, he's not that popular anymore." She leaned forward. "His column is barely read nowadays. It got canceled from the paper we both worked on last year. Heard he was hurting for money, too. Rumor has it he was writing some fancy-pants cookbook full of innovative and unusual recipes that he thought would make him rich."

Millie's brows shot up to her hairline. She looked at my mom. "Money? That's usually a motive for murder."

Mom opened her mouth, but before she could reply, footsteps pounded down the front stairs. Seth Chamberlain appeared in the doorway holding a plastic bag in his hand. Inside the bag was what looked like a small piece of paper.

"What's that?" Millie asked.

"We found this in the victim's room. Looks like he was writing some sort of a note. And since we discovered that he is a food-and-hotel critic, it isn't a big jump to assume the note was about the Oyster Cove Guesthouse." Seth held up the corner of an envelope. We could see it was part of a note, a few words scrawled on the edge. No, not exactly words, just parts of words. I could make out "ull" and "ick" and "son."

Millie craned her neck forward and squinted. "That doesn't look like a review to me."

Seth turned the bag back to face him. "Of course it's not the *whole* review. But anyone can put together that he was writing something about the inn being 'dull' and the food 'icky.' The killer clearly took the rest of it because they didn't want anyone to find it." His eyes drilled into mine. "And who wouldn't want someone to find a bad review about the Oyster Cove Guesthouse?"

"Lots of people," Mom chimed in.

"I didn't even know who he was until Ava mentioned it just now," I said.

Seth made a face. "You expect me to believe that? Your husband is a famous chef, surely you'd have heard of the Laughing Gourmet."

My expression turned sheepish. "I never really paid that much attention to what my husband said."

Seth didn't look like he believed me. I had visions of him whipping out handcuffs and hauling me off to jail. Millie must have had the same vision because she stood and went to Seth's side, possibly to distract him.

"Josie wouldn't kill anybody over a review. That's ridiculous." Millie patted his arm.

"People have killed for less, Millie. You're too nice." Seth beamed at her.

"Be that as it may, I have known Josie since she was in diapers and she is no killer."

Seth frowned and swiveled his gaze back to me. "What about that time she was caught trying to sneak out of the bowling alley with the rental shoes still on?"

Millie waved her hand dismissively. "Teenage hijinks. Besides, stealing shoes can hardly be compared to killing someone. I hope you're not getting any ideas about arresting Josie. That would be foolish. You have no concrete proof. This isn't even a letter, just some partial words. You wouldn't want to arrest the wrong person, would you?"

Seth considered that for a second, then said, "Maybe arresting the wrong person is better than arresting no person. We haven't had a murder in this town in more than a hundred years and I think the townsfolk will be nervous and want to know that the police are doing something."

"A false arrest will not gain their confidence and it will also ensure that I don't bake you any more of my blueberry pies." Millie let go of his arm and stomped back to her chair.

Seth's face fell. "Okay, fine. But if I get any more evidence that points to you, Miss Josie Waters, you won't have to worry anymore about what to serve for breakfast to your guests. You'll be getting served breakfast yourself. Too bad it will be bread and water at the Oyster Cove jail!"

That wasn't true. I happened to know they served eggs for breakfast there, but I was scared anyway.

Seth left and I exhaled. "Really? He was going to arrest me because of some partial words on a piece of paper? That's ridiculous," I said.

Was it possible that Charles was writing a bad review about the guesthouse? He'd been mad about the egg, but surely that wasn't enough to write a bad review? Even if it was, why would someone else kill him over it?

"Of course it is, dear," Mom assured me.

"We know you're no killer. But unfortunately Seth doesn't have much experience in murder cases. He'll want this wrapped up as soon as possible. There's only one thing for us to do."

"That's right." Mom pushed up from her chair and headed for the door. "We need to figure out who the killer is before Seth tries to arrest Josie again. The best place to start is the victim's room."

Chapter Four

Nero sunk his paws into the silky blue duvet on Charles Prescott's bed and fluffed. "Now that the police are gone, I hope the humans figure out they need to look in here for clues. If they don't come up soon, I'm game for a nap. This is my favorite room."

Charles had been staying in what Nero referred to as "the blue room." As you might have guessed, the room was a lovely shade of light blue. Nero found the combination of the powder-blue-and-gold silk oriental rug, Victorian-era, sky-blue flowered wallpaper and the robin's-egg blue silk bedding to be very relaxing.

The room also had all antique furnishings, handed down from Millie's ancestors, like the mahogany dresser and the four-poster bed. Nero loved the antiques because they were rich with lingering scents of lemon oil and pride from generations of use, unlike the new stuff that smelled like glue and a quick buck.

Marlowe poked her head in quickly from the adjoining bathroom. "I wouldn't be so sure that the humans will come. I don't think that redhead is too smart."

"You mean Josie?" Nero asked as Marlowe disappeared back into the bathroom to continue the search.

"Yeah, she said she *owned* us. She's clearly not too

quick on the uptake." Marlowe's voice was muffled, likely because she had her head in the trash can.

"She's just oblivious to the ways of felines. I sense that she has a kind heart and I think she's worth training." Nero hopped down from the bed. He'd already canvassed the room for clues and was waiting for Marlowe to catch up. He knew there was one whopper of a clue in the room and wanted to see if the younger cat could figure it out.

"Train her? You mean by not doing as she asks?"

"Naturally. And sometimes the exact opposite."

"Good idea." Marlowe trotted back into the room. She sat on her haunches, licking her front paw. "Okay. I noticed a scent that shouldn't be here."

"Indeed," Nero said. The young cat was coming along nicely. "And what do you make of it?"

"Well, it's salty like the sea but also has a tinge of seagull and wet dog. So, I'm guessing our victim was near the ocean and the gulls and possibly visited someone with a dog. Maybe near the cliffs where they nest or on the beach. Those darn seagulls are everywhere."

The mention of the gulls had Nero cringing. "Tell me about it. One dive-bombed me the other day and I had to do a tuck and roll right out in the middle of the street!"

"I had to hide under an azalea bush to get away from one."

"They're a nuisance."

"They don't even taste good. Like bland chicken."

"And very dry."

"Too salty."

Nero glanced out the window. The room had a partial view of the ocean and he could see the gulls flapping above the Smugglers Bay Inn. Good, let them stay over there. He didn't mind them so much if they just kept away from him. Live and let live, was his motto. "But still, they seem to be dying in droves. And I hate to think of anything dying before its time. They only have one life, you know."

"True." Marlowe sniffed at a pair of tan chinos that lay on the floor. "Judging by these pants our victim was up to something sneaky before he died."

Nero nodded. He had wondered if the other cat would discover the scent of nefarious intention on the human's pants. That was an advanced sleuthing skill and he was happy to see that Marlowe was mastering it. "What do you think our next move is?"

Marlowe raked her claws on the oriental rug. Millie would have a fit if she saw her. "We must talk to the gang at the wharf. One of them might know something about what our victim was up to." Marlowe started for the door.

Nero stayed rooted to his spot. The young cat would have to learn not to be so hasty. There was still something big left to be found. "Not so fast. There is another clue."

Marlowe turned back, her green gaze slit. "There is? I skulked around the whole perimeter of the room and didn't see anything that is not supposed to be here. Nor did I smell anything other than what I mentioned."

"Sometimes when looking for clues, it is not what you see, it's what you *don't* see," Nero said wisely.

Marlowe rolled her eyes. "Seriously? Could you be any more vague?"

Nero simply gave her a blank look.

Marlowe sighed. "Okay, fine. I'm making another round."

Nero watched the young cat carefully as she sniffed the perimeter, coming to stop in front of the small bookcase just as Nero had hoped. The bookcase was only two shelves that Millie had stuffed with a few old *Reader's Digest* volumes. It looked like Charles had put those all on one shelf and added his own books to the other.

Marlowe turned around triumphantly. "Aha! One book is missing."

Nero nodded. "Yes, and from the fact that the victim had kept books here in the first place, I think we can conclude that they were important."

"Yeah, I see that. So how are we going to alert the humans?"

"We'll have to draw their attention to it somehow. Naturally they will think *they* made the discovery."

"I know! We never get credit," Marlowe said. "But how should we draw their attention? Hairball? Incessant meowing? Leaping in the air?"

Nero watched as Marlowe pantomimed all of the above. He was proud that the young cat had figured out the clues, but she could be a little overzealous at times. "I think this calls for something more subtle. The good old pushing-everything-off-the-top-of-the-bookshelf routine should do the trick."

*

The police had secured Charles's room with a large "X" of yellow crime-scene tape. Was that really necessary? I worried that it would make the other guests nervous.

Millie must have had the same thought because she stopped in front of it. "Seems overly dramatic to have this here. What does he think this is, a scene from *Castle*?" She ripped the tape off one side, and Mom and I followed her into the room.

The first thing I noticed was that the duvet was messed up. It looked like something had been burrowing in it. A movement in the corner of the room caught my eye. The cats. I was sure Nero was the culprit. "If you have put any tears in that cover I'm not feeding you any more of that nice food with the gravy."

Millie frowned. "Josie! That is no way to speak to the cats."

As if understanding what she said, both cats trotted over to her purring and rubbing against her ankles while casting me angry looks.

"But they messed up the bed!" In my defense I had no idea how to talk to them. Should one let them just do whatever they wanted or was there some secret way to get them to obey you?

"You must never admonish or threaten them," Millie said. "That will only make things worse. You should speak to them as if they are the superior beings that they are."

The cats preened and purred.

I looked at Millie out of the corner of my eye. I wasn't sure if she had said that bit about superior beings for their benefit or if she was serious. If she was serious, then she was crazier than I'd previously considered. I filed that thought away for future reflection.

"Enough about the cats," Mom said. "We're in here looking for clues, right?" Her gaze fell on a pair of tan pants on the floor. "Look, the man couldn't even pick up his dirty laundry."

Now what in the world was I supposed to do with those pants? I had no idea what the protocol for dealing with a deceased guest's belongings was. Would the police come and take his things? Should I box them up? How long should I wait? Judging by the police tape that used to be on the door, I wasn't even supposed to be in here.

"I don't see any computer. That's usually where the good stuff is." Millie looked around the room.

"I don't remember him having one," I said. Had he? I thought back to when he'd checked in. He'd had a suitcase and a blue paper notebook but no case for a computer.

"Darn," Mom added. "Maybe he left another clue."

"I say we look in his bureau drawers." Millie opened a drawer and started pawing through it.

"I'll take the bathroom," Mom said.

"I guess that leaves the rest of the room for me." I got down on my hands and knees and peeked under the bed. There was nothing under there but dust bunnies. Not a surprise, I doubted Flora vacuumed under the beds. "Just what, exactly, are we looking for?"

Thud.

Over on the other side of the bed, something hit the floor. I jumped up to look. Marlowe was on top of the little bookshelf and apparently angry at the lack of attention. I'd heard that cats could be persnickety that way. She must have decided that a good way to get it was to push the little lighthouse statue off the top of the bookshelf.

"Hey now, kitty, that's not necessary for a supreme being such as yourself." I tried to temper my voice so it was soft and placating as I strode around the bed and picked up the statue. I was certain that cats responded to the tone of one's voice and not the words.

"They can understand sarcasm," Millie said from her position crouched on the floor looking in the bottom drawer of the bureau.

I smiled at the cat, who looked at me warily. I reached out to pet her and she hissed. I replaced the lighthouse and went over to the closet.

"No clues in here." Millie stood and brushed her hands together. "Maybe we should look in between the mattress and the box spring."

Thud. Mew.

We turned to see that Marlowe had now pushed a candle off the top of the bookcase.

"Is this some kind of behavioral problem I should be aware of?" I asked Millie.

"No, dear, they just love to push things onto the floor. Nothing is safe."

I replaced the candle. I could've sworn Marlowe rolled her eyes and looked at me like I was stupid. If you ask me, I wasn't the stupid one. Pushing things onto the floor when you knew someone would just put them back was stupid.

Nero was much smarter. He'd jumped up on the bed and was curled up on the duvet. "Please don't get cat hair on that." I tried to say it with the reverence due a superior being.

"There's nothing in this bathroom but shaving cream and toothpaste." Mom leaned against the door-frame looking disappointed. "How are we going to figure out why someone killed the guy if there are no clues in his room?"

Thunk! Merow!

Marlowe had pushed the alarm clock off the bookshelf.

"Now, Marlowe, really." Millie strode over to the bookshelf and petted the cat, who purred and bumped her head up against her hand. She bent to pick up the alarm clock but stopped halfway down. "Hey, this doesn't look right."

"What?" Mom and I joined her. I could see someone had rearranged Millie's *Reader's Digest* volumes and put different books in. "Ava told us Charles was writing a cookbook, maybe these are his books for reference or something."

Meow!

Nero had come over for his portion of attention and was rubbing the side of his face against the corner of one of the books.

"Huh, looks like there's a book missing," Mom said.

"Maybe he just didn't have enough books to fill up the shelf?" I suggested.

Millie straightened. "No, I don't think so."

Just then Flora sauntered past the room.

"Hey, Flora!" Millie yelled.

Flora stopped, backed up a few steps and narrowed her owlish eyes at us. "Oh, no. I don't clean crime-scene rooms. Anything with police tape I don't go in."

"We don't want you to clean." Millie pulled her into the room and dragged her over to the bookcase. "Do you remember if this shelf was full?"

Flora shuffled over to the bookcase and vertebrae cracked as she bent to examine the piece of furniture. She stopped with her face only inches from the shelf. She ran her finger along the layer of dust on the edge. "Yep, must've been something there."

"You remember that it was full?" I asked.

"Nah, my memory isn't that great. But look at the dust on the edge. If that spot had been empty, there'd be dust in there too, and that spot is clean as a whistle."

Chapter Five

Nero breathed deep, savoring the delectable aroma of rotting fish. The bait wharf was one of his favorite places in Oyster Cove. It wasn't just because the fishermen would sometimes throw them succulent scraps, either. The wharf had a certain ambiance that couldn't be found anywhere else. From the sounds of the waves lapping on the dock, to the briny scent of sea and the warmth of the sun warming his back.

It was heaven on earth...well, except for the seagulls. They were partial to the bait dock too and, as far as Nero was concerned, created an incessant nuisance with their constant swooping and cawing. A cat had to be careful lest he get knocked into the water. No cat liked that, except for Harry, who loved the occasional saltwater bath.

A shadow darkened Nero's path from above, and the loud gull cry made him cringe. He crouched, ready to dart under something, but the gull flew past. Looking up into the sky, Nero felt a tinge of sadness. There were fewer gulls than last week, and even though he wished they would go swoop somewhere else, he still didn't like the way their numbers were mysteriously dwindling. He didn't want them to die off, just to tend to their business elsewhere. Still, he was glad there were no dead gulls at the wharf; last week they'd seen a gull body floating in the water and it was a most unpleasant sight.

Milling about in their usual spot, behind a stack of lobster pots, were five cats. The largest one, a solid gray cat named Poe, was sitting atop an old lobster pot watching a fishing boat make its way out of the harbor and into the Atlantic.

On the ground next to the pot, Stubbs, an orange striped cat named such because his tail was a short stub, sniffed around the lobster pot for any old scraps of bait. The rumor about him was his tail had been chopped off with a cleaver when he'd been caught stealing an oxtail right from the butcher's shop, but Stubbs would neither confirm nor deny this.

Boots, a black cat with white paws and somewhat of a snobby attitude, sat in the sun grooming his whiskers, as he often did. His whiskers were elegantly long and thick, and they were his pride and joy. Nero had to admit they were lovely, but they were just whiskers after all. The way Boots carried on about them you'd think they were made of gold.

Harry, the large fluffy Maine coon, was flopped down in the sun snoozing while Juliette, a fluffy gray cat with a white diamond on her forehead, groomed her tail in a quite unladylike manner.

The cats stopped their activities as Nero and Marlowe approached.

"Heard someone got iced up at the guesthouse," Stubbs said. He was prone to using hard-boiled detective slang and Nero often thought that Stubbs's owner must read too many Dashiell Hammett novels aloud.

Then again, perhaps that was why the cat was such a good detective.

"Unfortunately, it's true." Marlowe trotted over to the lobster pot and peeked inside.

"Was it murder?" Boots gave his long whiskers an extra tug to emphasize the last word.

Nero's gut clenched. He was embarrassed that a murder had happened under his very nose. "Yes, it was."

"Did you see it happen?" Harry stretched, humping his back up with his front legs out in front of him before trotting over to sit in the circle the cats had formed.

Nero and Marlowe exchanged a guilty glance. "Neither of us was present at the time."

"So you don't know who the culprit is?" Poe asked.

Nero shook his head.

"How was it done? Poison? Gunshot? Stabbed?" Harry asked.

"Bludgeoned with a newel post," Nero answered.

"Nasty." Juliette shuddered.

"Who was the vic?" Stubbs asked.

"One of the guests at the inn. Charles Prescott," Marlowe said.

"And you didn't notice anyone unusual? Who's been hanging around there?" Poe asked.

"Well, there is Mike, Millie's nephew," Marlowe said.

"Oh, not Mike," Juliette said. "He's much too handsome. And besides, we all know Millie is one of the good ones and therefore Mike must be, too."

Poe frowned. "Yes, but what about the new one, Josie? Of course, we all love Rose and Millie, but Josie is an unknown. She's from away."

"She's not from away." Nero felt obligated to defend the new guesthouse keeper even if he wasn't exactly sure that he liked her himself. "She was raised here and moved away to raise her own litter. Now she's back where she belongs."

Boots quirked a brow. "So you two like and trust this new human?"

"Sort of." Marlowe ignored the warning look from Nero. "She did mention she *owned* us...she's not quite pet-broken yet."

Harry laughed. "*Owned you?* She's new to serving cats then?"

Nero nodded. "She sort of came with the house when Millie entrusted it to us. We still have much training to do."

"Have you tried the severed-mouse-head routine?" Harry asked.

"Not yet. We're still breaking her in."

"What about the pet-and-scratch routine?" Poe referred to the typical performance of acting like you wanted the person to pet you and then scratching them when they did.

"I've done that a few times," Marlowe said. "It seemed to put her in her place, but then she didn't want to pet me anymore."

"How about refusing to eat? So that she has to bribe you with tasty morsels?" Stubbs asked. "That one always sets the tone as to who is master."

"We might try that next." Truth was, Nero enjoyed eating too much to try that one. "Let's keep on task here. We must focus on finding the killer. If we don't, we may not be training Josie at all, or even have a guest-house to live in."

The cats nodded somberly.

"So you want us to do the usual? Keep our eyes open and scour the town for clues?" Harry asked.

This wasn't the first crime the cats had solved. Of course, the humans didn't realize the cats' involvement. Nero often thought it would be so much easier if humans would just be more aware. The humans' lack of cat-communication skills made the cats' job that much harder because they had to practically hit the humans over the head with clues to make them think it was their idea.

"Yes, but first I need to know if any of you saw anything out of the ordinary last night," Nero said.

The cats watched a sailboat glide past, cutting through the water silently as it made its way under the footbridge at the head of the cove and out past the jetty.

Finally, Juliette spoke. "It wasn't last night, but I saw a man up on the cliffs the night before that. It's quite unusual to see anyone up there, as the path is steep and treacherous." Juliette lived with their feline friend Julie at the rectory of St. Michael's Church, and often cat-napped in the belfry, which afforded a bird's-eye view of the cliffs. That was when the two cats weren't wreaking havoc in the rectory by spooling toilet paper off the rolls.

"Are you sure it was a man? It might have been Barbara Littlefield. You know how she mothers that lousewort."

The cats all made a face at the mention of the

noxious herb. Lousewort smelled like wet dogs and tasted even worse.

Juliette narrowed her luminescent blue eyes. "Of course I'm sure. I have excellent vision. It was a man and he was short, fat, and bald."

"That sounds like Charles," Nero said.

"And that would explain why he smelled like wet dogs and seagulls," Marlowe added. All the cats knew the seagulls nested near the cliffs and liked to eat the flockenberries that grew on the cliffside.

Nero nodded sagely. "Indeed, but what was he doing up there and why would that have anything to do with his death?"

"We'll have to sniff around town and see what we can dig up," Boots said.

"I'll listen in on Father Timothy's confessions. Perhaps the culprit will confess," Juliette offered.

"If only it would be that easy." Boots preened his mustache. "What we need to do is set our superior brains to thinking of the solution. Are there any other clues?"

"Only a missing cookbook," Nero said. "Oh, and it appears that someone was trying to cover up the crime and make it look like an accident. Someone had sabotaged the stairs at the guesthouse to make it look like the victim fell."

"And it almost worked except Nero here discovered the truth and we showed the clue to the sheriff," Marlowe said proudly.

"The sheriff does need a certain amount of...help," Stubbs said.

"That's why we need to get cracking on this." Nero swished his tail with urgency. "We need to find out if there was anything going on with the victim and someone in town. He must have been up to something to get himself killed. Can I count on you guys to scour the town, eavesdrop on all conversations and report back if you hear anything?"

"Yes!"

"Certainly."

"Of course."

"Consider it done."

"I'll start meow!"

"Good." Nero surveyed his gang of feline friends with pride. If there was something to be discovered about Charles's behavior, they'd ferret it out. He also knew the most important clues would be closer to home. "Meanwhile, Marlowe and I will go sniff around the guesthouse and see what we can dig up."

*

I didn't see any sense in doing something that would cause Seth Chamberlain to suspect me any more than he already did, so I was reattaching the crime-scene tape to the door when Ava Grantham came down the hall and caught us.

"Doing a little amateur detective work?" At first I was worried she might be the type who would tell the police that we were in the room, but her tone was laced with curiosity and her eyes sparkled with mischief, so I doubted she disapproved.

"No, the tape fell off and I was just reattaching it,"

I said, just in case my assessment of her attitude was wrong.

She surveyed us with narrowed eyes. "Uh huh..."

Millie didn't miss a chance to question another suspect. "Didn't you mention that Charles was working on a cookbook?"

Ava shrugged. "That was the rumor in newspaper circles. Why?"

"Well, do you see it in there?" Millie pointed to the bookcase.

Ava leaned over the tape for a closer look. "No, those are all already published. His wasn't published yet. He usually makes notes in one of those binders, you know the refillable kind that you used to use in school?"

"A three-ring binder?"

"Yeah, that's the one."

I glanced back at the bookcase. No three-ring binder. Maybe the police had taken it.

"We didn't find any binder in there," Mom said.

"I wouldn't be surprised if he just started that rumor to make himself look important and wasn't even working on anything. He was a washed-up old has-been." Ava leaned toward us and lowered her voice. "It's a mystery to me how the women still found him so attractive."

"They did?" I couldn't imagine anyone finding Charles Prescott attractive, and judging by the sour looks on Mom and Millie's faces neither could they.

"Yes, can you believe it? Of course he used to be a looker back in the day, but now...well, you saw him. Nothing to write home about. But I heard he still had a string of women." Ava glanced down the hallway, then turned back to them and lowered her voice again, this time to a whisper. "He even had one here."

"Here?" Millie looked aghast.

"Yep, I saw Tina coming out of his room late the other night."

"The other night? You mean the night he was killed? Are you sure?" Mom asked.

"I'm as sure as a monkey's uncle. But it wasn't last night. It was the night before. See, I'd fallen asleep in front of the TV in the sitting room and I was coming up the back stairs over there"—Ava pointed to the stairway at the end of the hall—"when I saw Charles's door open. I must confess, I ducked into the bathroom and hid behind the door because I didn't want to talk to him. But it wasn't Charles who came out. It was Tina."

"Did she say anything about why she was in there?" I still couldn't picture pretty Tina cavorting with Charles, but stranger things have happened.

"I didn't talk to her. I ducked back behind the door and I guess she just slunk off to her own room because I heard a door close, and when I peeked out the hall was empty. She never saw me."

Millie turned to me. "Did you get any indication that they were that chummy?"

"Not at all. It seemed like they didn't even know each other." I thought back to the interactions I'd seen between Tina and Charles. Charles had arrived four days ago, Tina had arrived the next day. Had they acted a little strangely around each other? It did seem like they'd made a point to avoid each other. Was I reading things into it because of what I now knew?

"Well, that is his modus operandi," Ava said. "He has a wife back home, so when he has these affairs, he just pretends like he doesn't know the girls. Oh, there were plenty of young girls at the papers we worked at years ago who were quite smitten with him. Though even then, I couldn't figure out what they saw in him."

"Tina did seem overly upset at his death, didn't she?" Mom asked.

Millie chewed her bottom lip and glanced back at the door to Tina's room. "Yes, she did. Was that because her lover had been killed or perhaps because she had killed him and was afraid of getting caught?"

"I wouldn't be so quick to pin the murder on her. She seems like a nice person and if you ask me, there are plenty of people who would've wanted Charles Prescott dead," Ava said.

Mom's eyes widened. "Really? You mean like old lovers?"

"Or his wife?" Millie asked.

"Not just them. Charles was a jerk. He wasn't above stepping on someone to get ahead, throwing a co-worker under the bus or even blackmailing someone if he had something on them. I say good riddance to him." Ava shot a sour look into Charles's room, then turned and strode down the hall.

We watched her go into her room before Millie turned toward the stairs. "Come on, we've got our work cut out for us. If what Ava says is true, we need to prove that there was a connection between Tina and Charles."

Chapter Six

"I didn't realize you were being so literal when you said we should go back to the guesthouse and *sniff* around." Marlowe lifted her nose from the flower bed and sneezed. "All this sniffing is making me hungry."

Nero gave an exasperated sigh. Marlowe still had to learn the art of patience. "We can eat soon. First, we must cover every inch. You never know where the killer might have dropped a clue."

"Right. Every inch." Marlowe stuck her nose back into the flower bed, then moved along to the corner of the guesthouse.

Nero continued on his course. So far he'd sniffed up several toads, a grasshopper, and a few gull feathers. The feathers gave him pause, but luckily the gulls didn't come over from Smugglers Bay Inn often, which was just fine with Nero.

He got a whiff of a familiar scent and looked up. He was on the east side of the house, where the wind whipped in from the ocean, causing the paint to peel. Millie had it repainted every two years. The mansion did need a lot of work, especially the old windows, which were no longer tight to the frames. The icy wind easily found its way inside in winter, especially on this side. During a nor'easter, the house could be downright frigid, especially if the power went out.

As Nero looked up, he saw that someone had fixed the window frames so that the windows were tight, and, according to what his nose was telling him, that person was Mike Sullivan.

"Looks like Mike fixed the windows." Marlowe sat down in the grass beside him. "I heard him tell Millie he was going to do it even though she didn't pay him to."

"He must have overheard Josie worrying about the heating bills come winter." Nero's heart swelled at the human's kind gesture. Mike must have done the work on his own time to help out Josie. Apparently not all people were selfish and uncaring. Maybe there was hope for humankind after all.

"Yeah, he's good people. And he gives good chin rubs."

Nero glanced at Marlowe sharply. "True, but you mustn't act like you enjoy them too much."

"Oh, I know. I give a few purrs of encouragement but jump off his lap just when he thinks I've settled in."

Caw!

A gull swooped overhead, and the cats ducked, crouching low while it flew past on its way to Smugglers Bay. Nero glanced over at the inn. Two gulls were circling above the deck. There used to be at least six. "Stella Dumont must be happy at the decrease in gulls."

"I'm sure she is." Marlowe continued sniffing along the side of the house. "I just hope our buddy Mike is smart enough not to fall for her."

Nero glared at the inn. They could see one corner of the building and the outdoor deck where Stella served meals to her guests. Nero wasn't above skulking around the edges of the deck looking for scraps, but not when the gulls were around. "She certainly does flirt with him, but do you think that's all she wants when she comes here?"

Marlowe followed Nero's gaze. "I don't know. She does seem very interested in the kitchen, but I haven't seen her do anything suspicious."

"Hmmm." Nero went back to sniffing. He didn't trust Stella Dumont, and not just because it seemed like she wanted to get her claws into Mike. She had a certain deceitful scent about her.

As Nero rounded the corner, he caught a foreign smell. Something spicy and uncertain. He closed his eyes and followed his nose, homing in until he was right on top of it.

He opened his eyes and blinked.

He was on the back side of the mansion's west wing. This side wasn't visible to anyone unless you were in the backyard, so Josie hadn't sprung for flowers and shrubs, but the gardener she'd hired had spread a thick layer of fine mulch up close to the building.

In that mulch was the unmistakable print from a shoe.

"You got something?" Marlowe trotted up and looked at the print.

"Yep." Nero glanced up. Right above the print was a window.

"Looks like someone climbed out that window

and stepped here in the mulch." Marlowe's whiskers twitched. "You know how damp it gets at night. The mulch was probably wet and the weight of the person compressed it. Then it dried into a footprint."

Nero was encouraged by Marlowe's deduction, but she'd missed one important point. "I believe you're correct. We need to get the humans out here right away so they can discover it."

Marlowe made a face. "I don't know. It could be from Mike or the gardener..."

"Don't think so," Nero said.

"Why not?"

"This is the west wing and if I'm not mistaken that window goes to the room Charles Prescott was killed in."

Marlowe's eyes flicked up to the window, then back to the mulch. "Then if that's true, that print could be the print of the killer!"

*

"Might be a good idea to pick something from my recipe file for breakfast tomorrow," Millie said once we were back in the kitchen. She was seated at the long pine table with a laptop open in front of her, googling Tina and Charles. Mom was eating one of the leftover lemon–poppy seed muffins.

"Therms-onsa-drough," Mom said.

"Huh?" I was a little worried at her unintelligible mumbling. Had Mom had a stroke?

She waved her hand in front of her face and made a big show of swallowing. "I said, these are very dry."

Millie's attention snapped from the laptop to the muffin. "They are?" She skewered me with a look. "The Oyster Cove Guesthouse prides itself on delicious breakfasts. I thought you were married to a famous cook?"

"Don't remind me." I hadn't absorbed any of Clive's extraordinary cooking skills, but so what? I was sure I could learn. Probably do a better job at it than him eventually, too. Though, judging by the way my mother was choking and gulping down water, maybe I'd better speed up the learning process.

Meow.

I glanced at the window. It was open, letting in a nice easterly breeze that carried the salty scent of the ocean along with the perfume of honeysuckle bushes that ran between the mansion and the old carriage house. Out on the lawn, Nero and Marlowe were trotting back and forth, looking at the house. I got the impression that they were looking right in the window at me.

Millie went back to her computer work, her eyes on the screen as she addressed me. "If the muffins are too dry, you need to add more fat. People think it means the recipe needs more moisture, but that's not the case. Try adding some extra butter or substituting buttermilk for regular milk."

Meow. Meow. Meow!

The cats' cries stole my attention again. They were getting louder, more insistent, much like when they'd discovered Charles's body. Hopefully they hadn't found another one. I looked out again. Now they were pacing back and forth.

"Have you fed them, dear?" Millie asked. "They like to have kibble left out in the morning and the wet food with gravy in the afternoon, and don't forget a treat at night." Millie glanced at the stainless-steel bowls on the black-and-white checkered floor of the butler's pantry—where we kept the cat bowls when Barbara Littlefield wasn't around. The bowls were empty.

"I fed them first thing. They must have eaten it all." I rummaged in the cabinet for the dry cat food and filled their bowls, then opened the screen door to call them in. They ignored me, running back to the corner of the house and then looking back at me.

"Give them time, dear, they rarely come when called. It's some kind of cat thing," Mom said.

Millie looked up from the computer. "Yeah, they'll come when they are ready. So, what are you serving for breakfast tomorrow?"

"I haven't decided yet." I was more interested in finding out if Tina and Charles knew each other, but Millie was typing so slowly I was beginning to wonder if that would happen in my lifetime.

Millie waved at the counter where the stack of cookbooks and recipes I'd inherited from her sat. "Now would be a good time to choose. Pick something out and I'll help you prepare it later."

Good idea. I leafed through the stack of recipes on yellowed index cards and worn scraps of paper, handwritten in blue pen that had faded so much over the years that the letters were barely legible. Combine that with splotches of food stains and I was starting to think I had more problems than my lack of cooking expertise.

Hmm...let's see. Quiche? Nope, I wasn't ready to tackle crust. Smoked salmon croissants? Too fancy. Eggs Benedict? Sounded complicated.

Millie must have sensed my dilemma. "How about my famous sour-cream coffee cake?"

I shuffled through the cards. A coffee cake sounded easy. Throw a bunch of ingredients in a bowl and bake. I didn't see anything with "Coffee Cake" marked on the top, but Millie's recipes weren't all labeled. "I can't find—"

"Eureka!"

Millie spun the laptop around to face Mom and me. "Look at this. Charles and Tina both worked for the *Daily Crier* in Noquitt, Maine, at the same time!"

I bent over to see the screen. Sure enough, there were articles from Charles and Tina. "Looks like Tina wrote a food column."

"Makes sense the two of them would know each other then, if they both write about food." Mom eyed the muffins again, but must have thought better of it, because she didn't take one.

"So we have our first suspect." Millie pointed at the computer screen proudly. "Tina had a secret relationship with the victim."

"Yeah but why would she kill him?" Mom asked.

Millie pursed her lips. "Maybe he wanted to break things off and she got mad."

"I don't know, Mike said the stairs had been tampered with as if the killer was trying to make it look like an accident, and that seems premeditated to me." I glanced out the window and saw the cats staring at me eerily with non-blinking eyes. Was that a signal that they were hungry?

"Maybe he told her earlier and she asked for a meeting so she could kill him?" Millie suggested.

Mom made a face. "You can't be serious. Tina is cute. Charles was old, bald, and pudgy. She'd probably be happy if he broke things off."

"And what about the missing cookbook?" I asked.

Merow!

Millie and Mom looked out the window to see Nero rolling on his back.

"I think Nero wants some of those salmon treats," Mom said. "Maybe Charles wasn't really even working on a cookbook."

"Right." Millie turned from the window and rummaged in the cat-food cabinet.

"And let's not gloss over the fact that Ava Grantham also knew Charles, and she's the one feeding us this information." I watched a lot of detective shows on television and knew the drill when it came to working out suspects.

"Good point," Mom said. "Maybe Charles spurned Ava at some point and she saw this as her chance to get even."

Meroop!

With a loud battle cry, Marlowe launched herself at the window screen, her claws out like razor-sharp grappling hooks. She clung on, her large round green eyes looking in at us, her belly heaving.

I jumped back, but it didn't seem to faze Mom or Millie. They simply stared at the cat as if this was a common occurrence. I certainly hoped it wasn't. After a few beats, Millie turned to me. "I think the cats are trying to get our attention. We'd better go see why."

Chapter Seven

By the time we got outside, Marlowe had unattached herself from the screen and the two cats were pacing around near the corner of the house. Millie tried to pet them but they darted off into the back. We followed.

Out back, the plantings I'd had the landscaper put in gave way to plain mulch. Funds were limited, so I'd only sprung for flowers on the sides of the house that were seen by guests. I wistfully thought of the day when I could have lush flowers all around the entire guesthouse. That was if I even *had* a guesthouse to landscape with all this murder business going on.

Another thing I couldn't afford was to fix up the old windows that were practically falling out. So imagine my surprise when I noticed the new wood around them. Someone had replaced the rotted frames and sills.

"Hmmm...I don't remember that being on my work order."

"I think Mike mentioned something about you losing a lot of air conditioning and heat through those windows come winter. My heating bill was through the roof last year," Millie muttered as she bent to pet Nero, who skittered out from under her hand and leapt into the bark mulch under the window.

"That's nice, but I can't afford to pay for this kind

of work." How much did something like this cost? I'd have to have a talk with Mike. I couldn't have him just doing extra work like this. I was on a tight budget and could only spare minimal funds for repairs since most of my money was needed for day-to-day operations.

"I believe he said it was at no charge," Millie said.

I jerked my attention from the window to Millie. "What? Who does work for free?"

"Someone who has a crush," Mom said, wiggling her eyebrows in a suggestive manner.

I made a face. "A crush? I think Mike's a little too old to have a crush." I was sure he wanted something, otherwise why do the work? Very few people did something for nothing. I couldn't imagine what exactly it could be, though. Was it possible that Millie was right and Mike had fixed the windows to be nice? My heart melted a bit at the thought.

"Never mind that." Millie waved her hand toward the windows. "This is the outside of the west wing and that one there goes to the room Charles Prescott was murdered in. I think the cats have found a clue."

Millie dropped to all fours and started combing through the grass.

Nero and Marlowe flopped down in the mulch, where they jumped, stretched, meowed, and rolled around. As I watched their antics, I noticed something in the mulch that looked odd. It was a depression of some sort.

"Wait a minute. Is that a footprint?" I pointed to the indentation and Millie crawled over.

"It is! It's a footprint!"

"Yeah but it's probably from Mike doing the windows," I said.

"I don't think so." Millie peered closer at the footprint. I half expected her to whip out a giant magnifying glass. "Mike wears work boots and this is not in the shape of a work boot. Work boots are more rounded and they don't have a high arch. But I know what does have a high arch. Chef's clogs."

Everyone looked at my feet. I was wearing chef's clogs.

"Come over here, Josie, let's see." Mom pulled me toward the mulch and I tentatively put a foot down a few feet away from the print.

"Press down hard to make the print," Millie instructed.

I did as told then lifted my foot. Sure enough, the print was very similar.

"Aha! It *was* a clue," Millie said as she reached down to reward Marlowe and Nero by petting their heads.

"Yeah but too bad it points to Josie," Mom pointed out. "When did you step in the mulch?"

"I didn't."

"I don't think it's from Josie," Millie said as she studied the print. "There's a bit of a difference. You can see here on the original print the edge is more rounded as if the clog is worn down, perhaps from someone who walks on the side of their foot. But if you look at Josie's print, the edge is sharp."

"So it's not Josie's print?" Mom asked.

"I don't think so," Millie said.

"I haven't been over here since the mulch was put down," I said.

Meow!

Marlowe scampered off to the other side of the house with Nero following at her heels. Apparently their job was done and they were off to greener pastures. Or at least I thought that was why they'd run off until I heard the booming voice behind us.

"Tampering with evidence?"

We all turned to see Seth Chamberlain standing there, his eyes flicking from Millie to my foot, which was hovering over the print I'd just made in the mulch.

"No. We found a clue. That's more than I can say for the police," Millie huffed.

Seth frowned, but his eyes regarded Millie softly. He came closer, then looked up at the window. "This is the window that goes to the room the victim was found in, isn't it?"

"Yes." Millie gestured toward the footprint. "And we found a footprint right here underneath the window. Now it seems to me the killer could've opened the window, climbed out and then shut it again. No one can see back here and he could have made the perfect escape into the woods."

Seth inspected the print.

"Uh-huh . . . Hmmm . . . Oh . . ." He looked up at us. "This looks like a print from a chef's clog. Are you sure you were discovering this clue and not hiding it?"

Mom fisted her hands on her hips. "Now, Seth Chamberlain, are you accusing us of obstructing justice?"

"Why on earth would we do that?" Millie asked.

Seth's eyes were glued to my shoes. "Well, this here is a chef's clog print and Josie there is wearing chef's clogs."

It figured that the only good thing I'd gotten from my ex-husband besides our daughter was chef's clogs. He'd always worn them and had talked me into trying a pair years ago. They were comfortable and I had taken to wearing them. It was only fitting that now, when I'd just started to get over our divorce and get my life on track, the clogs would be the thing that got me arrested for murder.

"Not exactly." I pointed to the impression I'd made in the mulch. "See my footprint from my clogs is shaped differently than that footprint there."

Seth squinted at the print and made a face. "Yeah I see, yours is fresher. The other one has been there longer. The edges are not as sharp."

"You can't be serious," Millie said. "Why would Josie climb out the window? She lives inside the guesthouse, so if she killed Charles Prescott, she would simply go back to her room inside the house."

"That's right." I nodded. "I mean, if I did kill him in that room. Which I didn't."

Seth looked dubious.

Millie put her arm through Seth's. "Now I know you do a thorough job, and don't jump to conclusions. Surely there are several other chefs who wear clogs and had a much better reason than Josie to kill Prescott."

"Yeah, like maybe the one he was writing that bad review about," Mom added.

Seth nodded, but still looked at me suspiciously. "Seems to me the bad review might have been about the Oyster Cove Guesthouse. I mean he *was* staying here."

"Yes, well, you're much smarter than we are at this sort of thing," Millie said, patting his arm. "I know you'll want to check out all the clues and suspects thoroughly before homing in on one particular suspect. You wouldn't want to arrest the wrong person, that wouldn't look good on your record."

"Of course not," Seth said, glancing my way again. "I also don't want to let the killer get away."

"Now, Seth, you can't seriously suspect Josie. And besides, where would she go? Josie owns the guesthouse. She's tied to the area. It's not like she's going to run off somewhere."

I nodded vigorously in agreement.

"What are you doing here anyway?" Millie changed the subject.

"Huh? Oh, I was coming to release the crime scene. We've got everything we need and I'm coming to take off the yellow tape. Personal belongings in there can be sent to the next of kin."

Millie's brows shot up. "Oh? And have you gotten any clues? Have you a list of suspects?"

Seth gave me another wary glance. "We're working on some angles, but I can't specifically say. Police business, you know."

"Indeed." Millie nodded. "And did you find a clue in Charles Prescott's cookbook?"

"Cookbook? We don't have any cookbook."

"You mean you don't have his notes for his new book that he was writing?" I asked.

"New book? We didn't hear anything about any new cookbook. Besides, what would that have to do with his murder? Seems to me that bad review likely ripped out of his hand is the thing that got him killed."

"Well now, I wouldn't be too sure." Millie pointed at the footprint. "Is it any coincidence that there is a chef's clog footprint right under the window of the room Charles Prescott was killed in and the man's notes on his new cookbook are missing?"

*

Flora's cleaning duties were limited, so after we got rid of Seth Chamberlain, I got to work, dusting, vacuuming, and toilet cleaning. You'd think that would've been the cue for Millie and my mom to leave, but it must have been a dull day down at the senior center because they stayed on.

For someone who wanted to be free to engage in retirement activities and not have to worry about the guesthouse, Millie sure still spent a lot of time here. But since she'd volunteered to prepare tomorrow's breakfast, I didn't complain, because that meant less work for me in the morning.

She was probably worried my lack of cooking skills was going to ruin the guesthouse's reputation for fine breakfasts. If a murder didn't ruin it, though, I hardly thought my cooking would.

It was late afternoon when I stumbled into the front parlor, exhausted. It had been a long day, especially considering I'd discovered the body of one of my guests that morning.

Flora was sitting on the overstuffed sofa in the front parlor watching soap operas and eating crackers. She glanced up as I flopped into a chair.

"I get a fifteen-minute break every four hours." She

said it as if I was about to chastise her for watching TV on the job.

"Lucky you, that's more than I get." I took off my clogs and massaged my aching feet. Who knew inn-keeping would be such hard work? When I bought the place from Millie she'd made it sound like others did most of the tasks.

Of the several parlors here, this one was my favorite because it was the sunniest. Golden afternoon light spilled in from the tall windows and turned the pine flooring to honey, brightening the already cheerful room.

Millie and Mom must have had the same idea. No sooner had I begun to relax when they trotted through the doorway with a tray full of chocolate-chip cookies. Millie set the cookies down on the marble-topped mahogany coffee table and both flopped into chairs.

"I think this new wrinkle in the case is going to help narrow down the killer." Millie bit into a cookie then pushed the tray toward Flora and indicated for her to take one.

"I certainly hope so. I don't like the way Seth keeps looking at Josie." Mom waited for Flora to choose, then picked her own cookie.

"Me either," I said.

"I think we need to find out what other restaurants Charles went to. If he was writing a bad review and the chef got wind of it, that would explain the footprint," Millie said.

"But what about the missing cookbook?" Mom asked.

"He may not have even been writing a cookbook," Millie said. "Ava said that herself."

"Speaking of Ava, I don't think she wears chef's clogs but I'm not ruling her out entirely," I said.

Mom leaned forward and lowered her voice. "Let's not forget Tina. If she was fooling around with Charles then that makes her a potential suspect. At least, that's how it always is on TV."

Flora remained silent, taking tiny bites of her cookie. Her eyes, gigantic behind the glasses, flicked back and forth from my mom to Millie to me as we talked.

Movement in the doorway caught our attention and we turned to see Mike, his broad shoulders leaning against the frame. "I figured if I followed the smell of cookies I'd find you."

He pushed off from the doorway, gave Millie a kiss on the top of her head, grabbed a cookie and sat in a chair.

"Were you looking for us or for cookies?" I asked.

"You, Sunshine. Thing is, I'm a little worried. There's a killer running around."

"Yeah, but the intended victim was Charles. The rest of us are safe." Millie leveled a look at Mike. "Right? I mean you're the ex-investigator, so you should know."

"It does look that way. Still, I think you all should be careful. Someone gave a lot of thought to planning out how to sabotage the stairs hoping the death would be ruled an accident," Mike said.

"Premeditated," Mom said ominously.

"Makes sense," Millie said. "If the killer knew he was writing that bad review, they probably planned to kill him before he had a chance to publish it."

"I don't know." I picked up a cookie and broke off a small piece. "Seems to me that killing Charles over the bad review would be something spontaneous, done in a fit of anger. The way the review was ripped up seems to indicate such."

"Maybe. Or maybe they ripped it up and then stewed over it until later that night, when they came back and killed him," Millie said. "The chef's clog print outside the window is the clincher. Maybe whoever it was killed Charles first and then got the idea to stage it after. I mean, that part of the house is closed off. They wouldn't worry about anyone stumbling across them while they were doing all that work."

"You found a clog print outside the window?" Mike glanced at my feet.

"It wasn't mine." I broke off another piece of cookie—bigger this time—and shoved it in my mouth.

"It was right under the window of that room," Millie said. "We think the killer escaped out the window."

"Which means it was not someone who was staying here," Mom added.

"That's possible, but whoever it was must have been here for a while because it would take them quite some time to stage the stairs to look like an accident," Mike said.

Nero and Marlowe appeared out of nowhere then, both jumping in his lap and purring loudly.

"No one would have seen them in there since that wing is closed. They would have had all the time they wanted to stage the stairs. But then there is the question of how they lured Charles into that part of the guesthouse. That would be hard for someone who wasn't supposed to be at the guesthouse to do," Millie said. "Maybe we should put more credence into Tina as a suspect. If they were having an affair, I could certainly see how she might use her feminine wiles to lure him there."

"They were having an affair?" Mike asked.

"Yes, please do try to keep up," Mom answered. "But if it was Tina then she would have just snuck back to her room. Why climb out the window?"

"Good question, and if it was Tina, then who left the clog print?" Millie asked.

Flora, who had remained silent the whole time, her head on a swivel like a referee watching a tennis match, spoke. "What about Stella Dumont?"

We all jerked our heads toward the window, where we could see the corner of the Smugglers Bay Inn, circling seagulls and all, in the distance.

"Stella Dumont? She does serve meals at her inn and it's possible Charles ate there," Millie said.

"I heard she was entering that cooking contest that the paper is running, you know, the one that has the five-thousand-dollar cash prize?" Mom said.

"She was? Well, that would be quite a coup for her business. If she won, she could use that to draw in customers, and, of course, the money never hurts." Millie stared out the window at the inn. "She does have that seagull problem, though. I wonder if her business is hurting."

"Maybe she's afraid the renovations Josie is doing will hurt it even further," Mike said.

"And maybe she's afraid a bad review from Charles Prescott would put her under," Mom said.

"She does a lot of the cooking over there; she might wear chef's clogs just like the ones that left that print under the window," Millie said.

"That might explain why she's been hanging around here," Flora said.

"She has? When?" I asked.

Flora shrugged. "I didn't write down the dates, that's not in my job description." Flora took another cookie and settled back in her chair. "But I saw her at the door by the kitchen a few times."

"The kitchen? What was she doing there?" I'd never seen Stella anywhere near the guesthouse and, given that we aren't exactly best friends, I doubted Stella would be popping over to pay a social visit.

Flora crunched on her cookie and looked up at us innocently. "I assumed she came here to flirt with Mike."

All heads swiveled in Mike's direction. Oh, that's right, he'd taken Stella to the prom instead of me. Sure, we'd just been kids and that was all water under the bridge now, but it spoke volumes as to his character.

Mike held his hands up in a placating gesture. "She doesn't come here to see me. But I have seen her in the kitchen a few times. I thought she was coming to see Josie."

I shook my head. "She's not coming here to see me. In fact, I had no idea she was anywhere near here. Did you talk to her, Flora?"

Flora shook her head. "None of my business what you people get up to. I see someone in the kitchen,

I figure they have a reason to be there. I don't ask questions."

"That's odd. What do you think she was doing here?" Mom asked.

Millie's eyes sparkled with excitement. She leaned forward. "Maybe she was casing the joint. Maybe she figured she could kill two birds with one stone. Get rid of the food critic that was going to give her a bad review and make it look like the guesthouse was unsafe, potentially getting it closed down, or Josie arrested for murder, and thus driving more business to her inn."

Chapter Eight

I wasn't going to sit around and wait for the police to accuse me again, so at five o'clock I headed across the field and down the hill to the Smugglers Bay Inn, hoping to catch Stella in the kitchen. I knew she served dinner at 5:30 p.m. so I figured she'd be in. It wasn't a social call. I wanted to see why she'd been hanging around the guesthouse and, most importantly, I wanted to see if she wore clogs.

I found her outside setting up the tables for dinner and waving her arms to shoo away the seagulls who circled around the deck. The deck overlooked the cove, and the subtle sound of the waves and scent of the ocean would have made for great dining ambiance if it weren't for the screeching birds.

"Shoo, shoo. Get out of here!" Stella flapped a white cleaning rag at the gulls. Two of them flew away, but one stood its ground on the post of the railing until Stella lurched toward it. She turned to glare at me as I approached.

I glanced at her feet. Darn it! She wasn't wearing clogs, she was wearing white tennis shoes. But that didn't mean anything. She could still be the killer. Maybe she had a pair tucked away in her closet, complete with telltale scraps of mulch stuck in the treads and splatters of blood on the top.

"Well, if it isn't Josie Waters. I heard there was an incident at your guesthouse. Hope that hasn't put off the tourists." Stella's tone indicated that she did indeed hope that very thing.

A gull swooped overhead. *Splat!*

A white-and-orange plop of seagull poop landed on the railing between us.

Stella raised her fists to the gull. "You get out of here!" She raced over to the post and wiped it clean with a napkin.

Good to know that she was just as subtle and lady-like as ever. And out here in the afternoon sunlight I could see that she wore just as much makeup too. A suffocating cloud of flowery perfume wafted over and I tried not to gag. She'd put the perfume on heavy in high school too. There was one difference, though— her hair hadn't been that bleachy shade of blonde back then. What in the world did Mike see in her?

I glanced back at my guesthouse. Maybe it was a good thing that I hadn't put in outdoor dining yet. Then again, I didn't have a problem with seagulls like Stella did. Her place was directly over the water, while mine was set back a bit, up on a hill with a panoramic view. Not only did the gulls circle her deck, I'd heard talk downtown that a few dead ones had been found on it as well. Nothing more unappetizing than a dead gull on an outdoor dining deck. Unfortunately, dead gulls weren't that unusual around here these days. The gulls seemed to be dying off at an alarming rate and their sad bodies had been found washed up on the beaches and even in the park downtown.

"Did you want something?" Stella came around the deck's edge toward me. "I would think you'd be trying to figure out who killed your guest."

"I am. Which brings up the question. Why do you keep coming over to the guesthouse?"

She frowned. "What are you talking about?"

"Don't play dumb with me." Actually, she didn't have to play, she *was* dumb, but I was less likely to get the truth if I let that slip out. "Flora said she saw you at the kitchen door."

Her eyes flicked in the direction of the guesthouse. "Well, I might have gone over a few times to see a certain person."

"So you've been lurking around the guesthouse to see Mike?"

"Mike and I are good friends." She leaned over the railing, a knowing look on her face. "*Very* good friends."

That figured. I wasn't surprised in the least. Except... if she really had been coming over to see Mike, why had he lied about it? He would have no reason to say he thought she'd been coming over to see me, unless he didn't want me to know that he was still carrying on with her. But why would he care if I knew? Someone was lying, that was for sure.

I crossed my arms over my chest. "So you really were coming over to see Mike?"

"So what if I was? It's none of your business."

"It's not. Well, other than the fact that a guest was murdered and you were seen lurking around."

"I haven't been lurking!" She waved the white cleaning cloth at the seagulls, who had resumed their circling.

"I'm very busy, if you must know. I have guests, gulls and other stuff going on. I don't have time to listen to your false accusations."

That's right, she did have "other stuff" going on. Like that cooking contest that would win her bragging rights and five grand. The contest that she might need an innovative and unusual recipe for. "You weren't interested in getting your hands on a certain cookbook, were you?"

"What? No?" Stella flapped the towel even though the gulls were gone. "Why would I want a cookbook? That's just silly."

Now that she seemed a little rattled, I figured I'd toss out another question. She might be flustered enough to give an incriminating answer. Though, honestly, I seriously doubted that Stella could pull off that kind of murder. Someone would have to know how to mess with the stairs to make it look like an accident, not to mention the sneaking in and out, and the planning. "Did you know the victim was a food critic? Maybe he ate at your place?"

Her eyes narrowed. "What? No. I didn't know anything about the victim. Look here, just because you got one of your guests murdered and you're jealous that Mike likes me better than you doesn't mean you can come over here and start accusing—"

Splat!

Seagull poop landed smack dab on the toe of her white tennis shoes. Darn, what a shame, she'd probably never get the stain out. Good luck for me, though, because it gave me another opening. "That's going to stain. You should probably be wearing your chef's clogs out here."

Stella had crouched to rub vigorously at her shoe. She scowled up at me. "Clogs? I don't wear chef's clogs. These sneakers are more flexible. Easier on the feet in the kitchen. Not that it's any of your business."

"I was just making a suggestion." I shouldn't be surprised she didn't wear clogs. Like I mentioned before, I didn't think she had the brains to be the killer. But something about her told me she wasn't telling the whole truth about why she'd been at my guesthouse. Mike hadn't seemed like he was lying. But why would Stella? But she didn't wear clogs, so that ruled her out as the killer. Unless she was lying about that too.

"Well, I don't need your suggestions." She scrubbed harder at the shoe. Just as I'd suspected, that stain was not going to come out easily. "If I were you, I'd pay more attention to your own inn instead of coming over here and trying to find out what's going on with mine. Maybe if you did, your guests won't need to seek accommodations elsewhere."

What was she talking about? Were my guests leaving now because of the murder? That's all I needed. No guests meant no income and no income meant failure. I just couldn't let that happen. And I certainly couldn't let it happen if it meant the guests would now be staying at the Smugglers Bay Inn. Was that why Stella had been lurking? Had she been poaching my guests?

"What are you talking about?" I asked.

She stood up, a nasty smirk spread across her face. "Oh, you didn't know? I'm sure I saw one of your guests checking in to the sleazy motel out by the highway. You know, the Timber Me Motel. They rent rooms by the hour. Too bad I'm full up or they could have come here where it's safe."

I reined in my temper. She was just trying to make me mad. I was sure she hadn't seen any of my guests there because no one had checked out. I crossed my arms over my chest and cocked my head to call her bluff. "Oh, really? And which guest might that be?"

"That ditzy blonde one. You know, the one that's in her forties but tries to look like she's a lot younger? Drives a black Volkswagen Beetle."

Tina? The description fit and Tina drove a black Beetle. She couldn't be talking about Tina, though. Tina was still registered with me. Sure, she'd taken Charles's death pretty hard, but not hard enough to move out. I hoped. "When did you see this?"

Stella looked up at the sky as if that's where she kept her memory—apparently we hadn't called her an airhead in high school for nothing. "Oh...two nights ago, I believe."

Ha! Charles hadn't even been killed yet. "Shows how much you know. The murder didn't happen until last night."

"Even worse. If your guests were already jumping ship before the murder, things weren't so great at your place then. Imagine what will happen now that someone's been killed."

*

Nero sat on the crest of the hill at the base of a tall Scotch pine watching Stella and Josie down at the Smugglers Bay Inn. He couldn't hear what the women were saying, but their body language indicated that the conversation was less than friendly. The sun was low in the sky, turning the wings of the gulls that flapped above the two women a brilliant white. The briny smell of the ocean mixed with the pine of the trees in a most pleasant aroma.

Beside him Marlowe was crouched with her front paws tucked underneath her, the sun warming her back. Stubbs, Boots, Poe, and Harry were also there. They were waiting for Juliette, who was commonly late.

"I don't trust that Stella Dumont." Stubbs's short tail twitched as he watched the two women with keen, intelligent eyes. "Never trust a dame who wears that much makeup."

"Me either," Marlowe said. "She's been lurking around the kitchen at the guesthouse and I saw her sneak across the field from her inn late one night."

"Didn't you say you smelled gulls on the victim?" Harry jerked his chin toward the gulls circling above the deck.

As the cats watched, one gull dropped a gift onto Stella's shoe.

"Looks like the gulls are good for something," Stubbs chuckled. "She'll never get that stain out of those canvas shoes."

"Stella Dumont might not be upset about the gulls' dwindling numbers." Poe pushed a gray paw behind his ear.

Boots looked up from his task of smoothing the spot on his chest where the white fur met with the black. "Do you think she could have something to do with what is happening to them?"

Poe shrugged. "I can't say."

"Doubtful," Harry cut in. "She's the type that doesn't like to get her hands dirty."

Nero decided to rein in the conversation before it got off track. They were here to discuss the clues in Charles Prescott's death. The reputation of the guesthouse was a more pressing matter to him than the fate of the gulls. "That is another mystery for us to solve later. Right now we need to get to the bottom of the death at the Oyster Cove Guesthouse."

"Sorry I'm late, guys." Juliette trotted up, her silky fur blowing back slightly in the wind like a supermodel at a photo shoot. "They had a lobster special down at Salty's Crab Shack and you know how the humans never take the time to get that succulent meat out of the tiny lobster legs. Billy tosses me the scraps in the back alley and I guess I lost track of time."

Juliette glanced down the hill at Stella and Josie, who were now glaring at each other in what looked like a human standoff. It was hard to tell with humans, their hairs didn't stand on end, their tails didn't stick up straight, and they didn't hiss or bare their teeth. But if they did, Josie and Stella would be doing that right now.

"Are they having a cat fight?" Juliette asked.

"Could be," Harry said. "We were just saying how we don't like Stella, and Marlowe has seen her lurking around the guesthouse, and Nero smelled gulls on the victim's clothing."

"You think she could be the killer?" Juliette asked. "Didn't Nero also smell dog?"

"I did," Nero said. "But Stella doesn't have a dog."

The cats knew every dog in a ten-mile radius, of course. It was cat 101 to know where canines lurked so they could avoid the unfriendly ones. Though not all dogs were unfriendly. Nero had even teamed up with one or two to solve cases at times.

Boots huffed and groomed his long whiskers. "I don't think her not having a dog comes into play. We've already determined the victim was up on the cliffs near both the gulls and the lousewort. That could explain both smells. We should be careful about jumping to conclusions at this early date."

"Yeah," Harry said. "We need a motive. Find the motive and it's easy to find the killer."

"And we need to evaluate all the clues thoroughly," Nero added. "Like the footprint in the mulch Marlowe and I discovered outside the window of the crime scene."

"A footprint? Do tell." Boots ran his paw along his long whiskers, making sure to twist so the whiskers curled up at the ends.

"It was a chef's clog print," Marlowe said proudly.

Everyone looked toward Stella and Josie.

Poe's green eyes narrowed. "Stella Dumont is not wearing chef's clogs, but Josie is."

"Perhaps we should take a closer look at Josie. I have an informant down at the police station. You know him, Stubbs," Boots said. "It's Louie Two Paws, the Siamese with the double paws. Anyway, he said that the victim was killed because of a bad review. That doesn't look good for Josie."

Nero huffed. "The police found a small scrap of paper in Charles's room. It's inconclusive as to what it really says. And besides, the review could have been about anyone, even Stella Dumont. Charles Prescott wasn't confined to the Oyster Cove Guesthouse, he ate at other establishments. The police are making assumptions based on the one piece of evidence that their inferior investigative skills have unearthed. Whereas we have found a chef's clog footprint, a clandestine affair, *and* a missing cookbook."

Boots nodded. "I suppose you are right. We must look at all the clues and let our superior brains determine who the appropriate suspects are."

"Well, I hate to say it," Stubbs said. "But Josie is a good prime suspect at least from the police's point of view. She had motive if the review is about the guesthouse, she had means because she lives right there, she had opportunity to kill the victim any time during the night and no one would think it was unusual that she was lurking around."

"No, it can't be Josie." Nero felt instantly protective of Josie, though he wasn't sure why. Surely he wasn't that attached to her. He'd only known her a few weeks. It was probably displaced loyalty for the Oyster Cove Guesthouse, which had been his home for several lives now. Millie had left the guesthouse to him and Marlowe, and they'd messed up by letting a murder happen in the first place. He had to make sure that whomever he accused was actually the right person.

Poe raised a brow. "Oh, so you are bonding with your new human, then."

"Maybe. Sort of. I mean she still needs a lot of work but it doesn't make sense that Josie would be the killer. Why would she kill him right in the guesthouse? That's sure to raise suspicion on herself. Not to mention that it's bad for business."

"And she is also looking for the killer. That's what it sounded like when we were in the living room earlier," Marlowe added. "And why else would she be at Smugglers Bay? She also suspects Stella."

Nero nodded. "Yes. Flora told her that Stella has been lurking around."

"But also, Mike said someone rigged the murder scene so that it would look like it was an accident."

"You don't say? A setup? Trying to make Josie the fall guy, perhaps?" Stubbs asked.

Harry gave him a knowing, skeptical look. "Or the sabotage could point even more toward Josie. Who else would have opportunity to be inside the guesthouse messing around with the murder scene without anyone thinking it was odd?"

"Right," Poe said. Then added, "Whatever was done to the scene probably took time and if it was not someone who was supposed to be there, questions would be raised."

"Not really," Nero said. "That part of the guesthouse is closed off. No one would be in there."

"Again, it all comes down to motive," Harry said.

"In my experience, the most predominant reason people get iced is one of two things: money or love." Stubbs shook his head as if to indicate his disappointment with petty human motives.

"That's the problem," Nero said. "We have both. We have the missing cookbook that one of his associates said could be worth a lot of money and we have heard a tale that he was having an affair with someone at the guesthouse."

Poe frowned. "Someone at the guesthouse? Who?"

"The blonde girl, Tina, or so Josie said," Nero replied.

The male cats all nodded knowingly.

Juliette frowned at them disdainfully. "That doesn't make very much sense. If it was someone at the guesthouse then why would they go out the window and leave the footprint?"

"Yeah, that's a good question. Why?" Marlowe asked.

Nero's gaze drifted to the cove as the cats considered the question. A red-and-white lobster boat bobbed in the waves. Inside, the lobsterman in his rubber apron was pulling up his pots. Nero watched as he snagged the blue-and-white polka-dotted buoy and put the rope on the wheel that would dredge up the pot. He recognized from the buoy colors—each lobsterman had his own color scheme—that it was Buddy Turner.

Nero liked Buddy because he was kind to the cats and usually tossed them his bait scraps. He hoped Buddy had a good haul. A few minutes later the wooden slatted lobster pot appeared. Inside, he could see the succulent little creatures, some sitting contentedly, others with claws flailing. Nero felt a momentary pang of sympathy for them, being dragged out of their environment and boiled alive, but it soon passed. They did taste good.

Finally, Juliette said, "Maybe the footprint is from someone other than the killer."

"Why would someone climb out the window?" Poe said. "It does not make much sense."

"I was merely considering all possibilities," Juliette hissed.

"What have you heard on the streets? Has anyone heard or seen anything?" Nero asked quickly to keep things on track, and also avoid a fight between the two cats.

Juliette fluffed her tail. "Unfortunately no one has come to Father Timothy to confess about the murder."

"Yeah, that would be too easy," Harry said.

"I did, however, notice some unusual activity from some of the guesthouse guests up on the cliff. The belfry offers amazing views." Juliette preened her tail. Nero suspected it was more to draw out the attention of her discovery than for actual grooming purposes.

"Who was it?" Nero asked.

"That older couple. The ones with all the cameras," Juliette said.

"The Weatherbys," Marlowe said. "What were they doing? It's a steep and treacherous climb up to those cliffs, and they are old."

"Tell me about it." Juliette's blue eyes narrowed in concern. "I was quite worried that I would witness them plunge to their deaths, as they were bandying about on the edge of the cliff with their cameras out. They are actually quite adept for older people."

"Seems awful risky but I guess you can get some good pictures up there on the cliffs," Harry said.

"Yes, it's a lovely view. Great backdrop for gull pictures," Juliette said.

Nero thought about this new wrinkle. Perhaps it meant nothing. The Weatherbys had said they were avid birdwatchers, and perhaps they would go to great lengths to get pictures of baby gulls, if there were any up there. With the gull situation going on, Nero wondered if they would be reproducing at all.

"So, the victim was seen up there. And the Weatherbys were seen up there." Boots's whiskers twitched.

"But if it was the Weatherbys, how does the chef's clog footprint figure in?" Marlowe glanced at Nero.

Nero simply tried to look wise. He had no idea how the two could be related. He didn't recall the older couple wearing clogs. He was sure he would have noticed and equally sure he'd only ever seen them in sneakers. But he supposed they could have a pair in their closet. Perhaps he should investigate. He didn't answer, though. He didn't want to seem like he had no clue. Part of his job of mentoring Marlowe was to appear as the wise teacher.

"What about the rest of you? Has anyone seen or heard anything?" Nero asked to avoid answering Marlowe's question.

Everyone shook their head except for Stubbs. "I might've seen something. I put a tail on the skirt. You know, the one you said was having an affair with the victim? In my line of work, you always follow the dame."

Nero's brows shot up. "And did she do something suspicious?"

Stubbs's shoulder sagged. "Not really. I spotted her

downtown and that's when I started the tail. She did a little shopping. Bought a purse. And then she went to the Marinara Mariner. I couldn't follow her in, of course, so I lost the trail."

"Why didn't you wait outside?" Harry asked.

"I did. I sat out on the sidewalk for more than an hour, but then the wife came out and shooed me away with a broom. She's a shrew! The owner, Tony, is nice, but that wife. Yeesh." Stubbs shook his head. "Anyway, I waited around back at the dumpster after that, but I never spotted her again. You can't see the front door from the dumpster and I didn't dare go back on the sidewalk with that wife around."

"Is it possible you were too busy looking at the contents of the dumpster to notice?" Juliette's voice was tinged with friendly sarcasm.

Stubbs drew himself up to his full height. "No. I kept watch the whole time."

"Perhaps you should've been tailing the Weatherbys," Poe said with an annoying air of superiority. He could be that way.

Stubbs made a face at him. "Maybe. I didn't know Juliette had seen them on the cliff and I was going on my instincts. What did *you* find?"

Poe simply pretended to preen his whiskers.

"You did the right thing." Nero glanced sideways at Poe. "At least you had some new information for us, though I don't see what it proves other than the fact that Tina likes to shop and eat. Too bad you weren't tailing her during the crime, then we'd know if she was the killer."

"But it doesn't all add up. What does the missing cookbook, the footprint, the affair, and the cliffs have to do with Charles Prescott's murder?" Harry asked.

"Perhaps we need to put our noses to the grindstone—literally. The sticky part is the footprint. The Weatherbys and Tina are both guests at the guest-house. Why would they climb out the window?" Nero mused.

"What about this footprint…did you scent anything on it?"

Marlowe glanced at Nero and he nodded for her to continue. Nero had picked up several scents, but he wanted to see if Marlowe had also. He felt a little bad he hadn't thought of this angle before. He'd been so focused on finding who wore the shoes, he hadn't con-sidered that the scents could lead them to a particular place.

Marlowe screwed her eyes shut and thought for a few seconds then said, "I smelled the usual things, bark mulch, anxiety, fear, but mixed in was another smell that I haven't smelled around the guesthouse. A flowery sweet smell with just a hint of bitterness."

Nero glanced at Josie and Stella, who were wrapping up their conversation. Josie was turning to leave.

"Was it cinnamon?" Juliette asked. "I smelled cinna-mon in the field between the Oyster Cove Guesthouse and the Smugglers Bay Inn."

Marlowe shook her head. "No, it wasn't cinnamon. It was more cloying. Like a flower."

"Hmmm, perhaps a flower garden?" Harry suggested.

"Maybe." Marlowe looked undecided.

"Well, I guess that's what we've got to work with," Nero said. "We need to explore all these angles. And put a tail on the Weatherbys."

The cats all stretched and turned to go in their opposite directions. Just as they were walking away, Poe turned around, his head cocked to the side, his green eyes thoughtful. "Oh, one more thing."

Nero sighed. Poe was always doing this. Saving up his little tidbit of information for the very last minute when they were all about to go their separate ways. But often Poe's little tidbits were vital to the case, so he tamped down his exasperation and patiently said, "What is it, Poe?"

Poe looked at Marlowe. "That scent on the footprint... was it sharp on the sweetness and tangy on the bitterness?"

Marlowe nodded vigorously, her eyes wide.

Poe nodded. "Well then, we might want to check the Marinara Mariner more thoroughly, because what you describe is very similar to the scent of saffron, and I happen to know that Tony had a saffron squid-ink pasta special running this week." Poe licked a paw. "It was quite delicious too."

Down the hill, Josie was starting back to the guesthouse. Nero thought about Poe's suggestion. Was it any coincidence that the chef clog had the scent of a special down at the Marinara Mariner and Tina was seen at the same restaurant? But did Tina wear chef's clogs? If she did, why in the world would she climb out the window after killing Charles?

Chapter Nine

It was a good thing that I didn't have to prepare supper for my guests because I was in no mood after that run-in with Stella Dumont. Where did she get off implying that the accommodations at a sleazy motel were preferable to those at the Oyster Cove Guesthouse?

Halfway across the field, I saw two familiar figures. Nero and Marlowe were bounding across the tall grass toward me from the path that led up the hill. I wondered what they had been doing up there.

They fell in step beside me. Unusual, because they usually ignored me. Maybe this was a good time to try to bond and make friends, like Millie had suggested.

"Where have you guys been?"

Nero looked up at me, his golden eyes almost glowing in contrast to his jet-black fur.

Meow. Merow. Meroop.

"Up on the hill, you say? Yes, lovely view up there." Was that the appropriate reply? I wasn't sure exactly how one spoke to cats. Surely they didn't understand the actual words, it was probably more down to tone and gestures. Did you talk to them like little babies? I glanced down at them. Nope. Not these two. Millie had said to talk to them as if they were superior beings.

Marlowe flicked her striped tail.

Meyou.

I had no idea what *meyou* meant but I decided to answer anyway. "Oh, me? I was over talking to Stella Dumont. Can you believe that she insinuated one of the guests had preferred accommodations in that sleazy motel out on Route One?"

Meooow!

Clearly Nero was as outraged at that thought as I was. "I know, right?"

We let ourselves in through the front door. I sauntered over to the guest register just in case Stella had been right. I didn't think she was, but it didn't hurt to double-check. I knew I hadn't checked out Tina, but maybe Flora or Millie had done it.

Tina was still signed in. I checked her folder and the bill was still open. She hadn't checked out. Take that, Stella Dumont!

Nero hopped up onto the desk and pushed at the register with his paw.

"Yeah, it's just as I had thought, Tina didn't check out. Stella doesn't know what she's talking about."

Nero blinked.

"But it makes me wonder…did Stella see someone who looked like Tina or did she lie? And if she did lie, then why?"

The guesthouse was extremely quiet. My stomach broke the silence with a growl so loud that it startled Nero, not to mention myself. It was unusual for the mansion to be this quiet. Normally I could hear the hammering and sawing that indicated Mike was at work, or the television, or guests talking. But it was past suppertime, Mike had gone home and it seemed that the guests were all out to dinner, as evidenced by the absence of their cars.

Just as well, I didn't really want company. I headed back to the kitchen, the cats on my heels and thoughts of my visit with Stella on my mind.

I rummaged in the fridge, pulling out a bedraggled slice of pepperoni pizza, a few muffins that were left over from breakfast, and the remains of the seafood dinner I'd had two nights ago. Two glass baking dishes with foil wrapped around the tops were neatly stacked in the back. A note from Millie indicated they contained broccoli quiche for breakfast the next day.

That reminded me, I needed to figure out what to feed the guests for the rest of the week. I glanced over at the counter. Hadn't Millie mentioned the sour-cream coffee cake?

I shut the fridge, to the protesting meows of the cats. "Don't worry, guys, I'll get your dinner in a second."

I opened a batter- and food-stained hardcover copy of *The Joy of Cooking* and leafed through the loose recipes stuffed inside. Some were on index cards, some ripped out of magazines, some just on pieces of paper. All in Millie's bold scrawl in fading ink. A smile tugged at my lips. I remembered some of these recipes from when I was a kid and had visited Millie here at the guesthouse with my mother.

As I leafed through the recipes looking for something that sounded tasty but looked easy, I chatted out loud to my feline audience.

"It's too bad Stella didn't have clogs on. If she had

I would seriously suspect her as the killer. Then again, maybe she lied about having clogs." I stopped the sorting and thought about that for a second. "I guess if she was the killer and wore the clogs, she might be afraid they had blood or some other evidence on them and lie."

Meow.

I pulled out a couple of recipes that looked interesting and put them on the counter. "And maybe she made that story up about Tina, but why?"

Mew.

"She probably just did that to be mean. She's like that, you know." I glanced down at Marlowe, who was watching me with her head cocked to the side. Did she give a little nod? I must have imagined it. "In high school she was one of those mean girls. Never could figure out what Mike saw in her. Not that I care. Is that why she keeps coming here, to see him?"

Merope.

"Why would Mike lie about that?"

Meow.

"I know. Men. Who can figure them out?"

I laid the recipes of interest on the countertop. I didn't find the sour-cream-coffee-cake recipe. I'd just have to pick something else.

"I suppose Stella could have been here for a more nefarious reason." I glanced in the direction of the Smugglers Bay Inn. I could see the gulls circling it from the kitchen window. The deck had been set for dinner, but no guests were out there. Maybe they stayed inside because of the birds.

Was it possible that bookings at the inn were suffering because of the gulls? Stella had entered that contest where the winner would get five grand. Was it for the prestige of winning or because she needed money? And if she needed money, then having the Oyster Cove Guesthouse shut down would mean more customers for her. But would she stoop so low as to kill someone?

And let's not forget that if Charles really was writing a new cookbook, then that book was missing. Had Stella somehow known about that and stolen it from Charles? What if that's why she'd been here and he'd caught her and a struggle ensued that ended up in the closed-off section of the guesthouse?

Nero jumped up on the counter and nudged my hand. Was that his signal that he wanted to be petted? But when I reached out a tentative hand, he let out a loud meow and almost scratched me. All righty then, here I was thinking that cat wanted affection but probably he was just getting impatient for supper.

"I know you must be hungry, but you have to get down from the counter. If Barbara Littlefield came in and saw you, she'd close me down!"

I bent down and opened the cabinet where I kept the gravy-style canned cat food Millie had said they liked. The recipes fluttered down onto the floor around me. Nero had pushed them off the counter.

I looked up to see him peering over the counter at me. "That's no way to get your supper."

Nero jumped down and batted at them.

"Hey, don't rip these, they're the only recipes I've got."

Nero sat back and I started putting the papers into a pile. The recipes triggered a memory of the ripped note the police had taken.

"Oh, that's right. That's the other clue. The review that Charles was writing. But was it really a review?"

Merooo.

I hadn't actually looked at the note in any detail, but when Seth Chamberlain had held that bag up I could see it was just a scrap of paper. Not even enough words to tell who the review was about. *If* it even was a review. Clearly the killer must've taken the other half. It seemed odd that the scrap of paper was found in his room, but Charles's body was in the west wing.

Had he fought with the killer in his room and then somehow gone down to the closed-off wing with them? That would indicate it was someone staying at the guest-house. Of course, it could have been a review about the Oyster Cove Guesthouse. But if it had been, then who had taken the other part of it and why? Seems like I would be the only one interested in keeping that from publication.

The piece of paper might not even be a review, but that didn't mean that Charles hadn't written a bad review of someone else recently. What if he had? And what if that chef heard he was in town and wanted to exact their revenge?

I glanced in the direction of the Smugglers Bay Inn again, except I couldn't see it because I was crouched on the floor. I didn't need to, though, because the thought was already in my head. If he'd previously written a review about Stella, maybe I could find it online.

I grabbed two cans of cat food in one hand and stood with the recipes in the other. The cans went onto the counter and I pulled out a recipe entitled "Brunch Egg Dish Casserole" that looked interesting. Bread, cheese, eggs, milk and ham. I had the ingredients for it. I could assemble it at night and pop it in the oven in the morning. If I wasn't mistaken, Mom had gotten this recipe from Millie and made it many times when I was a kid. It was quite tasty and seemed easy (at least it did when Mom made it). I put the recipe beside the cans and tucked the other recipes back into *The Joy of Cooking.*

Meow.

Marlowe had jumped onto the little table under the window that I used as a work desk and was prowling around my laptop.

"I'm one step ahead of you about looking online."

Mewoow!

I sat down and started typing. Turns out finding Charles's Laughing Gourmet reviews wasn't as easy as I thought. A search for the Laughing Gourmet brought up a website all about Charles, but when I searched for "Smugglers Bay" on it, no review came up. Odd, because I saw a few other reviews of restaurants in New York and Connecticut. I searched Yelp. No review was posted by him on there either. Charles probably didn't use common places where anyone could post a review, though. I decided to do a search on the Smugglers Bay Inn.

My phone chirped and I glanced at the display. It was my daughter, Emma. My heart filled with warmth.

As I answered, all thoughts of murder and bad reviews fled.

"Em! How are you doing?" I chirped.

"Great, Mom. What about you? Gram said there was some excitement in Oyster Cove today." Emma's voice had an edge of concern, and I wanted to put her at ease right away. As the parent, I was the one who was supposed to be doing the worrying, not her. Speaking of parents, what was my mother thinking telling Emma about Charles? Hopefully she hadn't mentioned that the excitement involved a dead body.

"Oh, a little excitement is always good. It's nothing to be worried about," I lied.

"A little excitement?" Emma sounded incredulous. "I would say a dead person is more than a little excitement. And I heard it was murder. Are you okay out there?"

Oops... apparently Mom *had* told Emma the details. The concern in Emma's voice made my heart swell, but I didn't want Emma worrying about me. I made a mental note to tell my mother to keep things like this under her hat. Not that I expected "things like this" to happen often.

"I'm fine. There's no danger. That poor man was killed over some sort of lovers' quarrel or old feud." I laughed to show just how unconcerned I was. "It's not like there's a serial killer running around town."

Was there? I had assumed that Charles's death was perpetrated by someone who had a reason to kill him, but what if there was a homicidal maniac running loose? For the first time I felt a niggle of worry. If the killer wasn't targeting Charles in particular, were the rest of us in danger? I pushed that thought to the back of my mind. Maybe I would be extra-cautious, but no attempts had been made on anyone else and Charles had had a reputation for rubbing people the wrong way. Hopefully his death was a one-off.

"Okay, Mom, but if you need me to come out there—"

"I wouldn't dream of it! You've got your new job." Emma had just finished college and was a rookie at the FBI Academy. Come to think of it, maybe I *could* use her help to figure out who killed Charles...but of course I would never involve her in something like this. Besides, I was a smart, confident woman on my own now and I didn't need anyone to bail me out. Not my ex. And not my daughter. I wanted to show her I could survive on my own, prove that I was competent and show her that women can do anything they set their minds to.

Mew.

Nero walked across the keyboard, his silky paws pressing the keys. I picked him up and put him on the floor but he just came right back and walked across it again.

"Okay, well, if you say so," Emma said.

"Of course. The police have it all wrapped up and there's nothing to worry about. How are things going at the new job?" I said, steering the conversation in another direction.

The murder took a back seat in my mind as Emma described the academy. I could tell by the enthusiasm in her voice that she loved her life. Part of me felt a little sad that she was all grown up and no longer needed me. She was living on her own and starting a promising career hundreds of miles away. But the other part of me was bursting with pride and happiness for her.

It was a constant chore to keep the cats away from the computer. Apparently they liked electronic devices, because they seemed to be taking turns either walking or lying on the keyboard and sitting behind the computer with their tails swishing on the screen.

By the time I hung up with Emma, I felt much better about the situation at hand. Emma was doing great and I'd persuaded her there was nothing to worry about here. Somehow just talking to her had filled me with confidence to figure out who had killed Charles, or at least to persuade the police that it wasn't me.

Meroo!

Nero stuck his tail in my face and I pressed my lips together and backed away. Yech. These cats sure got into everything. And they were starting to be pests with the way they were hanging around the computer. I'd never get any work done.

Prior to this the cats had mostly ignored me, but now their insistence on getting into my business was becoming annoying. It made me wonder if this relationship was going to work out. But I'd promised Millie, so I had to try. Maybe this was their way of telling me how hungry they were.

"I know you're hungry but if you'll just wait—"

Something on the computer screen caught my eye.

It was a review of an establishment in Oyster Cove,

but not the Smugglers Bay Inn. It was the Marinara Mariner.

Charles had eaten there last summer and didn't like the lemon meringue pie. It had been too sour for his taste and he used a lot of negative and colorful words to describe his disappointment. Words that might anger the chef. If I remembered correctly, Tony Murano, head chef and owner of the Mariner, had a bad temper. Did Tony also wear chef's clogs and hold a grudge?

Meow. Nero rubbed his head against me and I reached out to pet him. This time he let me. I glanced back at the screen. The cats must have inadvertently pressed a key that brought up this review on the screen. Ironically, the cat's annoying behavior on the computer had given me a clue.

"Yes, you did do good. I think a reward is in order."

Meowess!

I was hungry too and I'd left the cat food and scraps from the fridge on the counter. I pried open the white styrofoam takeout box and plucked out a shrimp. Nero and Marlowe sat at my feet staring up at the shrimp longingly as I popped it into my mouth. Cats liked shrimp, right? As I recalled, one of their favorite canned dinners was Scrumptious Shrimp Surprise.

"Okay, guys, you can have some."

Their tails swished excitedly as I put a few shrimp in each of their bowls, then set the bowls on the floor.

I leaned against the counter and listened to their contented purrs. As they chowed down, I thought, maybe this will work out after all.

*

"Maybe this relationship is going to work out after all," Marlowe said to Nero as she scarfed down her second shrimp.

"Agreed. Josie isn't so bad." Nero daintily bit into his treat. "But let's not forget we must not show too much enthusiasm for the human."

Marlowe looked up from her dish, a shrimp tail hanging out of her mouth. "What do you mean?"

"We wouldn't want to look too appreciative by gobbling down our food so fast."

Marlowe glanced down at the remaining shrimp in her bowl regretfully. Her whiskers twitched then she looked up at Josie, gave a disdainful meow and stalked out of the room, her tail high in the air. As she exited, she called to Nero over her shoulder. "How's that for not showing interest?"

"Perfect." Nero plucked the shrimp from Marlowe's bowl and downed it in one gulp before following Marlowe out into the front parlor where the comfortable overstuffed chairs were.

"I thought she was never going to get the hint with that computer," Marlowe said from her spot on the couch where she was curled up and washing behind her ears.

Nero jumped up onto his favorite chair, stretched, and then curled into a ball. "Thankfully she finally did. I thought she would never figure out the message I was trying to send with the recipes."

"Yeah, but you have to admit that was a hard one, and she did finally associate the recipes with the partial review that the police found, and that led her to looking on the computer."

"I suppose, it's just that she is so slow on the uptake." Nero tucked his face into his tail. "I think she'll come around, though. She has potential. I guess we still need to work on our communication. At least now she talks out loud to us."

"Lucky thing too because she uncovered a few more clues in her conversation with Stella Dumont."

"But can we trust the information?" Nero asked. "Stella Dumont isn't exactly a pillar of society."

"True, but I happen to know that Tina was not in her room late at night three nights ago."

Nero jerked up his head and looked at Marlowe. "The night of the murder?"

Marlowe sighed. "No, I said *three* nights ago. Two nights before the murder."

"Hmmm. I wonder if that is related...but why wouldn't she be in her room?"

"You got me. What about the rumor of her affair with Charles? Maybe they snuck off somewhere to be away from prying eyes?"

"Could be. The humans' love habits are strange and disturbing," Nero said.

"You can say that again."

"We should pay close attention to her." Nero looked out the window to see a Budget rental car pull up with the Weatherbys inside. "And let's not forget the Weatherbys. Clearly they were up to something on that cliff."

"Do you really think so? They are birdwatchers. And they're kind of old to be getting up to murder. If you ask me, they seem like the least likely suspects."

Nero looked at Marlowe sharply. "Never underestimate

the older ones. Look at Millie, she can do anything that people half her age can do. And she's smarter than most of them too."

"I suppose you're right. Sorry," Marlowe said. "We should be sure to follow all leads anyway. That's what you taught me."

Nero turned back to the window, a feeling of self-satisfaction washing over him. The young cat really did pay attention to him. He watched the elderly couple getting out of the car. They didn't look so elderly from here. In fact, they looked kind of spry. Cameras dangled from their necks as they hopped out of the car and practically sprinted to the front door, their heads bent conspiratorially together. "Yes indeed, we will need to watch the Weatherbys closely. Sometimes it is the least likely suspect that is the culprit."

Chapter Ten

The next morning, I slid the brunch egg dish casserole into the oven an hour before breakfast. It was piping hot and smelling fabulous when the guests arrived in the dining room. Breakfast was punctuated by the clink of forks on plates and the rustle of the breeze coming through the window. They talked in hushed tones. At least they were all there. No one had defected in the middle of the night to a different hotel.

I hovered near the mahogany buffet where I'd laid out Millie's breakfast quiche, orange juice that I'd juiced myself in my Jack Lalanne juicer, English muffins, a fruit bowl and, of course, coffee.

I was impatient for the guests to eat quickly and go. Mom and Millie would be here soon and I was eager to fill them in on the bad review and make a plan to visit the Mariner.

Today, Tina sat with the Weatherbys. They were still mothering her after yesterday's tragedy. Here they were, taking care of Tina out of the goodness of their hearts not knowing she could be the killer! At the very least she was sneaky, having had an affair with Charles and being seen creeping around his room. Funny, though, she didn't look like a killer with her innocent wide gaze and perfect complexion.

As I studied Tina, she daintily bit a teeny tiny morsel of the muffin. Was that how she stayed so thin? I glanced down at my waistline, which I liked to refer to as voluptuous. I wasn't fat, but I certainly wasn't thin. I was probably going to stay this size, because I doubted I could nibble an English muffin like Tina was doing.

She hadn't touched the rest of her food, either. Maybe if she had she wouldn't be so pale and wan looking. Was her appearance due to the stress of hiding that she was the killer, or was she just upset her lover had died? I still couldn't believe Tina would have the know-how to sabotage the stairs at the crime scene, as Mike had suggested.

Stella on the other hand...

"I say, Josie, you've really outdone yourself." Ava was sitting at the table next to the Weatherbys and Tina. She held up a forkful of the quiche and nodded at me.

"Thanks." I didn't feel the need to mention that it was actually Millie who had made it.

The Weatherbys stood, patting their mouths with the white linen napkins that matched the tablecloth. "Yes, quite delicious today."

Tina pushed some eggs around the plate with her fork. "It was, truly."

Mike appeared in the doorway, earning an appreciative glance from Tina—and also from Ava, if I was not mistaken. The Weatherbys nodded to him as they exited.

"Hey, Sunshine." He helped himself to coffee.

I rolled my eyes and faked a smile. "You must be almost done with your work here."

Mike sipped the coffee and made a face. I wasn't

sure if the face was about the coffee or the mention of his work. "Sort of."

"What do you mean? You have a set list of tasks that Millie paid you for. I don't have money for extras."

"The extras are on me. Seeing as we're such old friends." He moved closer. Too close really. Dizzily close. I stepped away, my butt hitting up against the sideboard. Ava watched from her table, a smile tugging at the corners of her lips.

"So, ummm...did you want something besides coffee?" I asked.

"Uhhh, yeah..." Mike glanced over at Ava then back at me. He lowered his voice. "The police tape is gone in the west wing and I wanted to show you something."

I glanced longingly back at the buffet table. I really wanted to clean up this stuff. But I also wanted to see whatever it was Mike had to show me. It might lead me to the killer's identity. Maybe a miracle had happened overnight and Flora would come in and clean up the breakfast dishes.

"Okay." I started toward the door and Mike followed, putting his hand on the small of my back. I sped up and his hand fell away. Who did he think he was? That was getting just a little too friendly and I didn't like the way my stomach tightened and I got all hot-flashy.

As we passed into the foyer, I ducked behind the little podium I used as a check-in desk to get the key to the door that shut the west wing from the rest of the guesthouse. The Weatherbys came down the stairs juggling various cameras and binoculars. When Ron Weatherby reached the bottom, he nearly dropped one of the cameras. Mike lunged to catch it before it smashed on the wood floor.

"Hey, nice Nikon." Mike admired the camera before handing it back to Ron. "Is that one of the new models that has the automatic close-up focus?"

Ron frowned at the camera. "Yeah, it's the newer model."

"So do you use it for close-ups of birds in the trees?" Mike asked. "Can you set the autofocus so it works in all lighting and situations?"

Ron glanced at Iona, then down at the camera again. "Yeah, that's just what we use it for. It took me a while to learn how to fiddle with all the dials and everything."

Mike's brows knitted together as Ron took the camera back.

"We're going out to do some birdwatching on the beach." Iona smiled and tugged Ron toward the door.

"Have a great time," I said.

Mike watched them leave, an odd look on his face. "That was strange."

"What do you mean?" I asked.

"Well, his answer about the camera was kind of odd. There aren't any dials to fiddle with on those."

"Really?" I watched them hop into their car and drive off. "Well, they are old, maybe he didn't know what he was talking about or couldn't remember or used the wrong words?"

Mike shrugged. "Maybe. Come on, let me show you what I found in the room."

We proceeded down the hallway to the west-wing door. I was glad to see it was still locked. Barbara would have approved, though I was sure she'd find something else wrong to complain about. I opened it and we stepped inside. The room had a creepy stillness to it. My stomach tightened as I glanced over at where Charles's body had been. You could make out all the footprints in the dust and a dark stain. Blood? I was sure Flora would say that cleaning blood was not in her job description.

"Look over here." Mike pointed to the stairway where several of the treads had been broken. The small section of the railing that was left dangled precariously. It had appeared at first that Charles had slipped, perhaps grabbing at the railing, which gave way, causing him to tumble down the stairs and hit his head.

"Looks like the stairs collapsed," I said.

"It *looks* like it. But, if you look closely, you can see that the stairs were sawn from underneath." Mike got down on his hands and knees and gestured for me to follow suit. He tilted his head to the side to look at the treads from below. I did the same. I had to get very close to him to see what he was pointing at. There was definitely something fishy going on underneath those stairs—and it wasn't the way Mike had gotten me on my hands and knees so easily either.

"You can see how they sawed away just enough so that a light amount of weight would cause the stairs to break. But they didn't cut all the way through, so at first glance the wood is splintered like it rotted and gave way. But when you look closer you can see the even break underneath."

I looked again. He was right. "Do you think the killer did this before and somehow persuaded Charles to come down the stairs?"

"Maybe."

I glanced at the pile of railing spindles. "But then why hit him with the newel post?"

"The fall probably didn't do the trick. Or it's possible the killer bludgeoned him first and then set the stage to make it look like Charles had fallen by accident."

"But wouldn't someone have heard something?" I gestured toward the boards. "I mean, all that sawing makes noise, right?"

Mike rocked back on his heels and looked thoughtful. "It does. But it's possible the person did this some time ago and the sounds were masked by renovations going on in the other part of the house. Who can really tell where hammering and sawing noises are coming from? And I've been working pretty steady every day, so the killer would have had plenty of opportunity."

"So that means it wasn't just done in anger when someone saw he had written a bad review." If only the police would see it that way, maybe Millie wouldn't have to promise Seth Chamberlain so many pastries not to arrest me. I glanced over at the window. "We found a footprint outside the window. I think the killer might have escaped through there."

I thought about Tony Murano, my stomach taking a tumble. Charles had written a bad review about Tony's lemon meringue pie. But if Tony was the killer that meant he'd planned this all out ahead of time. And that he'd come to sabotage the stairs and then lured Charles in here. Maybe it wasn't such a good idea to go to his restaurant. Then again, what could he do to me in broad daylight?

Mike walked over to the window and looked outside, then checked the lock. "It's unlocked. You know you should keep all the windows locked here, Sunshine.

Oyster Cove might be a nice town but there *is* a killer running around."

I refrained from rolling my eyes. *There he goes again treating me like a little sister.* I remembered it from when we were younger. I hadn't appreciated it then and I didn't like it very much now either.

"Maybe the killer unlocked it to get out. He wouldn't have been able to lock it back up once outside." So there, Mr. Smartypants!

"Good point." Mike walked back to the stairs. "Whoever did this went to a lot of trouble to make it look like an accident. They must be angry that we weren't fooled."

"And nervous about being caught." I walked back to the staircase and got on my hands and knees to take another look at the sabotage just to make sure that it really had been done on purpose. "It looks like you'd have to know exactly where to cut to get the boards to break like this. Who would know that?"

I had been intent on studying the saw marks and hadn't realized that Mike had crouched down beside me. His voice startled me. "Anyone who knew about carpentry, or building."

I glanced sideways at Mike. "Like you?"

Mike looked incredulous. "Why in the world would I sabotage the stairs and kill your guest? I didn't even know the guy."

"He might have pissed off someone you're close to. Someone whose been lurking around here." I glanced in the direction of the Smugglers Bay Inn. Not that I really thought Mike would kill someone for Stella, but stranger things have happened. And besides, what about the clog print? Maybe they'd done it together and Stella had hopped out the window in her clogs.

Mike caught my drift and his scowl deepened. "You think I did this for Stella Dumont? No way. She might have been interesting in high school but believe me, I have no designs on her. I'm older and wiser now and prefer my women... not quite so made-up."

He reached out to pluck a cobweb out of my hair and I suddenly felt self-conscious about my lack of mascara or blush. I had put a little lip gloss on this morning, though, so hopefully that counted for something.

Self-consciousness gave way to guilt. It wasn't fair to accuse Mike. I had no evidence and he had been nothing but nice since working here. Even if his kindness was suspicious, it was not suspicious enough for me to accuse him of murder.

"Sorry. I don't really think you killed him."

"I guess we should tell Barbara Littlefield about this." Mike leaned forward and looked underneath the stairs again. "She's been running around town saying this place is unsafe."

"I know. I have no idea why she has it in for me. I'm trying to restore it to the way it was originally. You'd think she'd be happy."

"I don't think she's ever happy," Mike said. "But it might be *me* she has it in for."

"You? Why would she have it in for you? And why would getting the guesthouse closed down hurt you?"

Mike shrugged. "I guess she doesn't like anyone doing any kind of renovations or improvements. Wants things to stay just the way they are, and since I've been back in town, I've been doing a lot of renovations. Not to brag, but I am getting kind of popular in the home-improvement sector."

"No doubt. But why focus on the guesthouse? I don't see what it has to do with you."

"She probably thinks that casting a cloud on the work here would dissuade people from hiring me. Plus, she knows I'm attached to this place because of Aunt Millie. But I think she's just crotchety in general. She doesn't like that I came back here after a career in the navy and started taking up carpentry. Thinks it's suspicious."

Now that he mentioned it, it was a little suspicious. Why would a navy guy be doing carpentry?

As if reading my thoughts, Mike continued, "I always liked working with my hands and now that I've left the navy, it gives me something to do. It's not about the money. I really just wanted to help out Aunt Millie." His gaze drifted and locked on mine. "And now you."

Footsteps sounded in the hallway. "Hey, look, this door is cracked open, I thought Josie was supposed to keep this wing locked."

The door swung in and we looked over our shoulders to see my mother and Millie. Their eyes scanned the room, then widened as they fell on Mike and me kneeling on our hands and knees before the staircase. Millie's eyes widened. "Oh, sorry. We didn't mean to interrupt." They backed out and Millie started to pull the door shut behind them.

I leaped up. "You're not interrupting anything."

They stopped and looked at us skeptically.

"We weren't?" Mom's left brow was quirked up as

she nodded toward the stairs. "Looked like you were doing something to me."

"Yeah, you young people, one never knows what you're getting up to. You do things differently than when we were young," Millie added.

Mike stood and brushed the dust off his hands. "We weren't up to anything. We were looking at the staircase. Someone sabotaged it so that it would be unstable."

"Oh, really?" Millie hurried over and plopped down onto her knees. I was surprised she could do it so easily. "Let me see."

My mother joined her. Maybe they took yoga or something? The two of them seemed to have no problem getting around on all fours.

"Oh, I see. Right there, Millie." Mom pointed to the part of the treads that had been sawn.

Millie looked back over her shoulder at Mike. "What do you make of it?"

"Someone wanted to cover up the murder," Mike stated the obvious.

Millie smiled proudly and glanced at me. "My Mike was an investigator in the navy. He knows about this stuff. You should listen to him."

"I'll try to keep that in mind," I said. I probably wasn't going to listen to him, though, in fact, I was counting the days until he wouldn't even be around.

"Well, well, well. I guess your suspicions were right after all, Mike." Millie stood. "So we have the chef's clog, the missing cookbook, the torn review, and now the sabotage."

"And don't forget the illicit affair," Mom added.

"Affair? Cookbook?" Mike's eyes darted from Millie

to Mom. "You ladies wouldn't happen to be investigating again, would you?"

"Who, us? No. We're just little old ladies with too much time on our hands. One has to have a hobby, you know."

Mike crossed his arms over his chest, disapproval radiating from his velvety brown eyes. "Investigating is not a hobby. It can be dangerous. You ladies should not be meddling in a murder case."

"Don't be silly, dear." Millie waved her hand. "We're not meddling."

Mike looked to me for support. "Don't you agree, Josie?"

I glanced at Mom and Millie. I actually did agree that they shouldn't be meddling. But Seth Chamberlain had me at the top of his suspect list so someone other than the police had to investigate. I knew they weren't going to stop either, so I figured it was best if I got in on the ground floor. "Don't worry, I'll make sure they don't get into trouble."

Mike looked skeptical.

"That's right. You don't have anything to worry about," Millie said. We all stood around and looked at each other for a few beats, then Millie continued, "Well, don't you have some work to be doing? I'm not paying you to stand around."

Mike rolled his eyes and sighed. "Okay, fine." He gave me a pointed look. "But I'm counting on *you* to keep them in line."

He kissed Millie on the top of the head as he left.

"He's a dear boy, but such a killjoy sometimes. Honestly, you young people seem to think we're doddering old fools who can't take care of ourselves." Millie brushed dust off the front of her shirt.

"Indeed. I think they forget who raised them." Mom glanced at me. "So, what's going on, Josie? I can tell by the look on your face that there's something else. Spill it."

I looked out the door to make sure Mike wasn't lurking around in the hall before speaking. "I did find out something else last night. Charles Prescott wrote a bad review last year about the Marinara Mariner."

Millie's brows inched up. "He did? Now that *is* interesting. And if I'm not mistaken Tony Murano is one to hold a grudge."

Mom nodded vigorously. "Yes, he is. Remember last year how he almost got into a fight with Vinnie from Vinnie's Pizza because he thought Vinnie stole his marinara recipe?"

Millie nodded. "Who could forget? And even when it turned out he was wrong, Tony wouldn't even apologize."

Mom pressed her lips together. "And I bet Tony wears chef's clogs."

We all glanced at the window.

Millie whipped out her phone. "There's one way to find out for sure."

She thumbed into the phone like a teenager. After a few seconds she squinted at the thing, then nodded and smiled. "All set. We have a reservation for one o'clock at the Marinara Mariner. Come on, Rose, let's go see if Vera can fit us in at Tremulous Tresses. I think I need my roots touched up before we confront the suspect."

Chapter Eleven

I had some time to kill after I cleaned up the breakfast dishes and fed the cats—who did not act at all appreciative of the shrimp I'd given them the night before—so I decided to head downtown. It would be closer for Mom and Millie to meet me there anyway and I wanted to visit my best friend from high school, Jen Summers, who worked at the post office.

Another good thing about moving back home was that I'd had a chance to reconnect with Jen. We'd been inseparable when we were younger, but had drifted apart when I'd moved away. It was hard to stay in touch while raising kids and all, but now that the kids were out of the house and I was back in town, we had a lot of time to catch up and I stopped in whenever I could.

The post office was the epicenter of Oyster Cove's rumor mill and Jen always knew everything that was going on in town. But I wasn't going there to pump her for information, I was going for the emotional support.

The Oyster Cove Post Office was in an old brick building in the center of Main Street. It had been built in the 1920s and no one had thought to do a thing with it since. It still retained the old marble-checked tile floor, oak teller windows with bars, wainscoting on the bottom half of the walls, and the pervasive smell of stamp glue. I had to admit, it had a certain charm.

Jen looked up from her job of stuffing the mailboxes as I entered. A smile replaced the bored look on her face and she practically dropped the mail on the floor to greet me.

"Hey, how's it going? I heard you had a murder at the guesthouse! I hope you're okay out there."

Her expression was a mixture of interest and concern. I was touched that she was concerned about me but figured she also wanted to know all the details. Clearly I was okay, since I was standing right in front of her.

"I'm fine. It's terrible that someone died but, even worse, I think Seth Chamberlain might suspect me."

"Pfft..." Jen waved her hand in the air. "I wouldn't put any stock in what he says. Remember when we were in high school and he kept trying to catch us with our boyfriends at Makeout Point? He was pretty easy to pull one over on."

She was right. It hadn't been hard to evade Sheriff Chamberlain when we were younger. But now..."That makes me even more nervous. If he's so incompetent, he might arrest me just because he can't find the real killer."

Jen gnawed on her bottom lip. "Oh, yeah. True. So, tell me what you know."

I told her about the partial note, the affair with Tina, the missing cookbook, the sabotage, and the clog print. "And Flora said that Stella Dumont has been hanging around the guesthouse so, naturally, I suspect her."

Jen nodded. "She's sketchy and I heard she needs money."

"You did? I did too. Mom said she entered some

cooking contest and when I went over to question her, she acted evasive. You ask me, those gulls that keep pooping on her deck are hurting her business."

"But why would that make her kill your guest? Do you think she wants to make it so people are afraid to stay at the guesthouse?"

"Maybe. She acted like she had a reason to be there."

"What reason?"

"She implied she was there to see Mike Sullivan, but then he denied it."

Jen made a face. "Hunky Mike Sullivan? What would he want with Stella? I'm sure she was making that up. She's not the most truthful person, you know."

It was true that Stella was prone to lying. "Yeah, but I'm not sure I trust Mike either. Whoever sabotaged that room had carpentry knowledge."

"Oh, come on. Mike wouldn't do that. He's a nice guy. Please tell me you aren't still holding a grudge about what happened back in high school?"

My spine stiffened. "Of course not. That would be so immature. I couldn't care less about Mike Sullivan. But, like I said, the crime scene was altered by someone in the trade and if the shoe fits…"

"Speaking of shoe, you found a clog print and Mike doesn't wear clogs. My money is on Stella."

"Stella wasn't wearing clogs when I visited. She claimed she doesn't wear them ever, but she could be lying. There's another person who might fit that clog print too." I told her about the review I'd seen on the lemon meringue pie. "I'm meeting Mom and Millie to go there for lunch at one."

"Lordy, you have your mom and Millie in on this?"

"Not much choice. Those two get into everything."

"Are you regretting your decision to move back here and keep an eye on your mom?" Jen wheeled a cart over and started sorting mail.

"She is a handful, but no. I love it here and buying the Oyster Cove Guesthouse was the right move. Even if it did take my life savings."

It was only partially true that I had moved back here to keep an eye on my mother. Daddy had passed on five years ago and at the time I'd been terribly worried that my mother would wallow in grief. Luckily, she'd adjusted to widowhood like a trooper. Now I was worried about her barging in on crime scenes and causing trouble with Millie. It was like I'd turned into the mom and she into the teenager.

But the other reason I'd moved back was that I'd been terribly hurt by Clive. I'd left that marriage feeling like I was worthless. In order to soothe that pain, I'd run back to the one place where I'd always felt safe and secure. Oyster Cove. And buying the guesthouse gave me a way to rebuild my self-worth. Well, as long as I could be successful at it, and I doubted this murder was going to help with that.

"And then it's all made worse by Barbara Littlefield running around town telling everyone we should be closed down because the house is unsafe. So if Chamberlain doesn't arrest me for murder, Barbara Littlefield might close me down. Either way, there go my savings down the drain."

Jen clucked in sympathy. She knew how important it was for me to make a go of this on my own. "Don't worry, no one listens to Barbara. She's always grousing about something."

"Right, except as the building inspector, she does have a lot of power."

"I wouldn't worry about Barbara," Jen assured me. "She doesn't like change but she just wants to make sure the town doesn't get too built up. She comes off as a hard-ass, but she has all our best interests at heart. The tourists come for the quaint ambiance of an old-fashioned Maine fishing town and she wants to make sure that's what they get. She'd never close down the guesthouse, it's part of the town's history."

"I suppose."

"She's just crotchety." Jen tossed some mail into the cart. "But you have to give her credit for finding the Furbish Lousewort and working to get the government to declare that a protected area. Otherwise they would have built that big hotel. That would have changed the town forever. And not in a good way. Probably would have put the guesthouse out of business."

"Yeah, I guess." I hated to admit I might owe Barbara one for stopping the construction. I knew she hadn't done it for me, but Jen was right about the hotel.

"You hang around long enough, you might be able to thank her in person." Jen pointed to a pile of packages. "She gets a lot of packages. Some of them are dirty."

My eyebrows shot up. "You mean she gets porn?"

Jen looked at me and laughed. "No. Dirty like with dirt. I don't know, she might get special fertilizer for that lousewort, you know how she babies it."

"Oh, that kind of dirt. For a minute there I thought

maybe I could have some sort of blackmail to leverage over her."

Jen made a face. "Eww... just the thought of Barbara and porn makes me glad I had a light breakfast."

"Ditto."

"So what about this Tina person? Do you think she could've done it? Lovers' quarrel?" Jen asked.

"I really have no idea. She was very upset when we discovered the body, but she could've been acting," I said. "I just can't imagine her being with Charles. I mean she's kind of pretty."

I glanced out the window to see a seagull perched on the back of one of the benches they had set at intervals on the sidewalk. They were picturesque with barrels of flowers beside them. The gull made me think of Stella Dumont. "And I still don't know why Stella's been lurking around the guesthouse."

"Does she have a connection to the victim?"

"I'm not sure. I couldn't find anything. When I looked online the only review I found was the one for the Marinara Mariner. She sure was acting suspicious yesterday, but she was distracted because the gulls were flocking around her deck like she was putting out a buffet for them."

Jen glanced out the window. "Yeah, what about the gulls? It's weird what's happening to them, isn't it?"

"For sure. But Stella probably isn't unhappy about it. They congregate around her deck and I don't imagine her guests appreciate them begging for scraps when they are dining outdoors."

"I don't know. I think some tourists like to feed them. That's how they got in the habit of stealing sandwiches out of their hands on the beach in the first place."

"Hmm…" I glanced at the gull who appeared to be watching people as they strolled past. Probably sizing them up for a culinary handout. "Maybe people have stopped feeding them and that's why they are dying off."

Jen shook her head. "I don't know, Gordon Swift from the Audubon Society was in here the other day saying something about experts looking into some kind of a disease."

"Oh. Well, that's not good. I hope it doesn't spread to other animals." I thought of Nero and Marlowe. Could cats catch a disease from seagulls? I certainly didn't want something happening to them.

"Anyway, it can't be that they're starving. They eat those flockenberries up on the cliff. That's why they poop orange, you know? The berries are orange and pass right through," Jen said. "And there are tons of those berries. Those things are invasive. They practically choke out anything else nearby. Mrs. Landsdowne had them in her garden and they killed all of her tomato plants."

"You don't say." As I made a mental note to make sure I didn't have any flockenberries in the gardens that I'd be redoing at the guesthouse, something on the street caught my eye. It was my mother and Millie dressed to the nines and making a beeline for the post office. "Looks like I better get going. Millie and my mom are coming and it looks like they're dressed to kill for our lunch at the Marinara Mariner."

*

Despite its kitschy name, the Marinara Mariner was a pretty decent upscale Italian restaurant. It was located a few doors down from the post office and had a definite Tuscan vibe. The hostess led us through the dimly lit room, across the clay-tile flooring, through the arch and into a grotto area with one wall made out of large stones and the others painted a pleasing Tuscany mustard color.

We were seated at a cozy table in the back. Our water glasses sparkled under the chandelier, our silverware gleamed. The plates were simple white china with a gold rim and the acoustics were such that we could only hear muted snatches of the other diners' conversations. I could tell Mom and Millie were straining to eavesdrop on Carolyn Wheatly and her boss, John Collingsworth, who looked particularly cozy in the corner.

Even the menu was classy, all done in dark-brown quality faux leather with nice printing inside. I scanned the items—antipasto, eggplant, veal—while inhaling the tang of tomato sauce and freshly baked bread.

"What are you going to have, Josie?" Millie looked at me over the top of her menu. "It's my treat."

"I can't let you do that, Millie." Though it would be nice because I didn't really have any money for eating out. I scanned the side dishes. Maybe I could make do with a side of broccoli?

"Don't be silly. I'm rolling in it now that I have all that money from the sale of the guesthouse." She leaned across the table and lowered her voice. "And besides, if we play our cards right, we won't have to pay a dime."

Worry set in. Mom and Millie were known to play

fast and loose. My eyes narrowed. "Just what are you two planning?"

"It's nothing bad." Mom put down her menu. "I'm having the lasagna."

"I'm going for the veal scallopini. What about you, Josie?" Millie asked.

"Salad. Now tell me exactly what you are planning to do?"

Millie pressed her lips together and looked over my shoulder at the waitress who had appeared with a pitcher of water. Saved by the waitstaff, but it was only a temporary reprieve. The waitress would have to leave sooner or later, though it looked like it would be later given all the questions Mom and Millie were asking about the food.

Finally, after they found out about every dish, ordered what they wanted and demanded a basket of rolls, the waitress left.

We spent a few minutes chatting about the decor and then I resumed my inquisition. "Okay, fess up, ladies. What do you have planned? How are you going to figure out if Tony Murano is our clog-wearing killer?"

"Why, we have to look at his feet, of course." Millie fluffed out her napkin and deposited it in her lap with a flourish.

"And just how do you propose that?" I asked.

"Oh, don't worry, dear, we know how to get an audience with the chef." Mom looked over the edge of her water glass at me, her eyes sparkling with delight.

"How do you do that?"

"Why, we complain about the meals, of course." Millie looked at me as if I was daft. "Shhh…here they come."

The waitress deposited the plates on the table and we tucked in. Millie and Mom both felt sorry for me and insisted I try theirs. It was delicious.

"I don't see how you can complain about this food, it's delish," I mumbled around a mouthful of lasagna.

"Oh, no?" Millie passed the glass of light Pilsner she'd ordered to Mom. "Hold my beer."

"Oh, miss. Miss..." Millie flapped her hands in the air to summon the waitress, who hurried over with a frown on her face.

"Can I help you?"

Millie pushed her plate away from her. "This veal is as tough as shoe leather!" Never mind that she'd eaten almost all of it.

The waitress looked at the plate skeptically. "I'm so sorry, can I get you something else?"

Millie folded her arms over her chest. "Certainly not. I'd like to see the chef."

"I'm sorry, but Chef Murano doesn't leave the kitchen." The waitress looked a little scared but I wasn't sure if it was of Millie or Chef Murano. If rumors of Murano's temper were true, it was likely of him. All the more reason to suspect him of the murder.

Millie harrumphed. She sat up straight, her eyes shooting daggers at the waitress. "But I insist. Nothing will make this better except a visit from Chef Murano himself. I demand to see him."

The waitress's eyes narrowed slightly as if she was going to call Millie's bluff, but she must have thought better of it because she simply said, "I'll see if he's available," before scurrying off.

Millie's scowl turned into a smile. She grabbed the beer from Mom and took a swig. "See. Works every time."

Millie's gloating was short-lived. The waitress came back wearing an apologetic look.

"Chef Murano is busy in the kitchen. He said to offer a free dessert."

"Free dessert?" Millie said loudly, her voice incredulous. "That's no compensation."

People were starting to stare and the waitress looked antsy. "We can take your meal off the bill..."

Millie shot up from her seat. "No. None of that will do. I need to talk to Chef Murano. Which way to the kitchen?"

"You can't go in th—"

But Millie was already marching toward the steel doors that clearly led to the kitchen, casting a follow-me glance over her shoulder at us.

Mom tossed her napkin on the table and slid out of the booth. "Guess we should go with her."

The kitchen was a flurry of activity and a chaos of smells. Pots clanged, sous-chefs rushed around plating salads and putting dollops of whipped cream on desserts. In the middle, Tony Murano stood in front of a steel table. He was tall with dark hair, a five o'clock shadow on his chin—though it was only 1:30—and hairy knuckles. Perhaps I noticed the knuckles because they were clutched around a cleaver that he held high in the air. The fluorescent lighting glinted off the blade as it sliced down toward the table.

Thwack!

Mom, Millie, and I all jumped as the cleaver cut through the side of beef that had been lying on the table.

"Oh!" Mom gasped.

Tony's eyes jerked from the beef to Mom, then me, then Millie. His face darkened. "What are you doing in here?"

Millie marched to the other side of the table. I could see her trying to peek over to see what he had on his feet but she was too short. "I would like to complain about my veal."

Tony's eyes narrowed. The cleaver glinted. "Look, lady, there's nothing wrong with the veal. I tasted it myself. I think you're just trying to weasel out of paying the bill."

"I certainly am not!" Millie stomped her foot then tried to peek around the corner of the table. "I just wanted you to…umm…" She turned around and looked at us.

"Admit that the meal was subpar." Mom came to her rescue.

"Subpar? Who are you people? Food critics? I don't like food critics." Tony raised the cleaver and we all took a step back.

The sous-chefs had stopped working and were watching the argument.

"We are not food critics." Millie started around the corner of the table, glancing back at us with a knowing look. "We're just little old ladies trying to get a good meal. Social Security only goes so far, you know, and we need to get good value for our money. But, more importantly, we want you young people to have the manners to admit when something isn't good."

Tony was looking at Millie like she was a three-day-old salad. Clearly he didn't want to be on the same side of the table as her because he sidestepped away.

"Listen, lady, you need to leave."

Millie pressed her lips together. Clearly this tactic wasn't working. "Well maybe a handshake then and we'll call it a day?"

She started toward him but Tony held up the cleaver, stopping her.

A door in the back of the kitchen burst open. A woman stood in the doorway, her eyes narrowing as she took in the intruders in the kitchen. She glanced from Tony to Millie to Mom, her eyes widened when they got to me.

She looked furious as she turned to Tony. "What's going on in here? Who is *she*?" She jabbed her finger in my direction.

Tony scowled. "I don't know, honey. They burst in here demanding I apologize because they didn't like their dinners."

The woman, Tony's wife or girlfriend apparently, looked like she didn't believe him.

While Tony was distracted with this woman, Millie sidled over to the other side of the table. She craned her neck looking down in the direction of Tony's feet. Her eyes widened and she glanced over at us nodding her head in an exaggerated manner. Honestly, she couldn't have been less subtle.

Luckily, Tony was no longer paying attention to us. He was busy arguing with the woman who was now standing in front of him, her hands fisted on her hips.

"Well, I certainly hope that this hussy here isn't trying to get your attention." She jerked her head in my direction. *Hussy?*

I raised my hand. "Uhh...I just came with them. I don't want anyone's attention."

The woman got in Tony's face. "Is that right? Maybe she came here thinking I wasn't in and she could have you all to herself."

Tony took a few steps back. "No, dear, that's not it at all." He swaggered away from the woman toward us. When I say swaggered, I don't mean in an old-fashioned cowboy way. I mean that he had a funny way of walking on the sides of his feet. Just like the clog print we'd found in the bark mulch.

Continuing with her subtle methods, Millie gasped and pointed at his feet. Luckily Tony still wasn't paying attention. I mean, he did have a cleaver in his hand.

Millie scurried over to us and grabbed Mom by the elbow. "Well, looks like our business here is resolved."

Tony scowled at her, the cleaver glinting off the light. "What do you mean, lady? I thought you were mad about your meal and wanted some kind of lame apology. Which you aren't getting."

"No worries, I can see you have good intentions." She tugged Mom toward the door. "So all's good then. See you later!"

And with that Millie turned and dragged Mom out of the double doors.

I had just enough time to throw some money on the table for the bill and a tip and meet them outside on the sidewalk.

Millie was already halfway down the street, her heels clacking on the sidewalk. "Well, I guess that settles it. Tony Murano was wearing the clogs and he walks on the sides of his feet. He's the killer!"

Chapter Twelve

"Anybody want the crusty garlic bread?" Harry asked from his perch on the edge of the dumpster.

"I do," Juliette said.

Nero watched as Harry used his tail for balance while reaching one orange-striped paw into the dumpster to skewer the garlic bread, which he flipped to Juliette, who pounced on it.

A piece of newspaper drifted out and fluttered to the ground. Nero noticed it was the food section. "I hope there are no reviews in that paper from Charles Prescott."

"Like the one the police found in the victim's room?" Harry tossed out a cheeseburger and Poe claimed it as his own.

"Yes and we also made another review discovery last night," Nero said.

"Do tell?" Boots wiped some marinara off his whiskers and sat on his haunches.

"Well, I think we finally made a breakthrough with Josie," Nero said.

"It took her a while to get our drift, though." Marlowe looked up from the remains of the shrimp scampi she was chowing down.

"Some humans can be a little slower than others,"

Juliette said. "Father Tim took a long time to get on the same wavelength, but I think he's coming along fine. Don't give up on Josie."

Nero and Marlowe exchanged a glance. "Oh, we won't. In fact, last night we were able to guide her toward something very interesting on the Internet."

"What?" Boots asked.

"It was actually Josie who instigated it; she's not so bad after all. I think she has some smarts," Marlowe said. "She was looking for reviews for the Smugglers Bay Inn thinking that Stella Dumont might be mixed up in this."

The cats all nodded. "Yeah, she could be a killer."

"No, she's too stupid," Harry said.

"Sometimes they only play stupid and they're really crafty," Stubbs added.

"Would you let them tell us what they discovered?" Poe asked.

"It was a review for this very restaurant." Marlowe licked scampi sauce off her nose.

"The Marinara Mariner?" Juliette asked.

Nero nodded. "Indeed, it seems Charles did not like a pie that he was served here."

Juliette scrunched her nose up. "Was it the lemon meringue? It *is* very tart."

"Yes, I agree." Harry hopped down from the dumpster with a slab of eggplant.

"Well, that is very interesting." Boots's whiskers twitched.

Harry swished his tail. "Tony had the saffron special the other night and saffron was smelled on the clogs outside the window."

"Are you sure it was saffron that you smelled?" Poe asked Marlowe.

"I don't know, I never smelled saffron," Marlowe answered.

"Me either," Nero added.

"Hold on." Harry jumped up on the rim of the dumpster and leapt right in. The sides clanged as he rummaged around, jumping out with a small napkin in his mouth. He dropped it in front of Marlowe. "There's a little bit on the napkin."

Marlowe and Nero looked down to see an orange smudge. They sniffed. Nero's eyes widened. It was the smell. "That's it all right."

"Well, there you have it," Poe said. "Tony got a bad review. Tony's footprint was outside the window of the room where Charles was murdered. Sounds like a wrap to me."

"You think that dame I followed here has anything to do with it?" Stubbs asked.

"Tina?" Juliette asked. "Probably just a coincidence. I mean, lots of people eat in the restaurant."

"Probably. And I admit that all of this with Tony sounds suspicious, but what about that old couple, the Weatherbys?" Harry said. "I followed them around just like we suggested and you'll never guess where they went."

"Where?"

"Right up to the gulls' nests. They were practically crawling in them."

"Why would they do that?" Stubbs asked.

"Birdwatchers. Some of them can be quite eccentric,"

Poe said. "But it makes me wonder. Charles was up on the cliff. The Weatherbys were up on the cliff. The gulls are up on that cliff. Could the gulls have something to do with Charles's death rather than a bad review? And if so, why was Tony's footprint outside the murder room?"

*

When we got back to the guesthouse, the guests were either out or in their rooms, which was a good thing because Millie couldn't stop blabbering about Tony and his cleaver.

"He could've whacked any one of us right there in the kitchen!" Her words echoed through the foyer as she dug out her phone.

"I hardly think he would've done that in front of all the witnesses," Mom said.

"Either way, I'm getting Seth to come right over and we can tell him about our interrogation." Millie dialed and put the phone to her ear.

"I'd hardly call it an interrogation," I said. I was nervous about what Seth might say. Would he be mad that we went there? Would he feel threatened that we'd tried to do his job? But it was a little suspicious that Tony wore clogs and walked on the sides of his feet. It would seem to indicate that the print matched, but how reliable was a print in bark mulch? I could already picture Seth pointing out that any number of weather conditions could've altered the print. If the bark was too moist maybe his feet sank at a different angle. It was hardly conclusive. Then again, we had the bad review to back us up.

"I need you to come over right away. I know who the killer is!" Millie yelled into the phone. Unfortunately, she did this just as the Weatherbys were coming in.

Iona gasped. "Did she just say she knows who the killer is?"

Ron fumbled his camera, practically falling down the last three steps. "How would you know and not the police?"

"We're really not sure." I tried to usher them toward the stairs before Millie started talking about cleavers and chopping up people. "We think we might have some clues based on something we found here at the guesthouse."

Iona's hands flew to her face and she and Ron exchanged a glance. "Oh, dear, it's not someone staying here, is it?"

"No, it's someone else," I assured them. Clearly they were very nervous about having a killer in their midst. I felt a little guilty about suspecting them earlier.

Their relief was obvious. Iona took Ron's arm and propelled him toward the stairs. "Well, that is a relief. Let's go freshen up and then we can go back out and have a nice afternoon of birdwatching. The sun is out and the birds are twittering and if you're catching a killer, all the better!"

It took Seth Chamberlain only ten minutes to arrive on the scene.

He looked at Millie skeptically as she explained everything that had happened in Tony's restaurant.

"And just how did you come about going to the Marinara Mariner?" he asked. His arms were crossed over his chest and he wore a disapproving scowl on his face, even though his eyes turned soft as marshmallows whenever he looked at Millie.

"Because of the review, of course." Millie glanced at me.

"I found a review that Charles had written on the lemon meringue pie at the Mariner last year and it wasn't very good," I explained.

The furrow between Seth's brows deepened. "Last year? Why would Tony kill him now?"

"Maybe he just found out that Charles was in town?" Mom suggested.

"Seems highly unlikely. Why would he carry a grudge all this time? Not to mention that he'd have to come all the way over to the Oyster Cove Guesthouse, sneak inside and then kill Charles." Seth shook his head, his eyes cutting over to me. "Nope, it seems more likely that the person he was writing that review about found it in his room. They probably ripped it up before they killed him. And it seems more feasible that someone here would be the killer."

That made me a little mad. Up until now I was cutting Seth some slack. I mean, he was a friend of Mom and Millie's, and he seemed like a nice old guy, but now he was getting me a little angry with his not-so-subtle looks in my direction. "We don't even know if he was writing a review. All you found is a scrap of paper with some words on it. And by the way, don't you know me well enough to know I'm not a killer?"

Seth's face reddened and he looked down at the ground. "Well, Josie, I knew you when you were a kid. But you've been away all these years."

"I'm still the same person."

"She has a point about the review. Let's see what it said again," Millie said.

"It's pretty obvious, look." Seth pulled his cell phone out of his pocket and scrolled to a picture of the paper he'd had in that bag.

He held it up and we all craned our necks and squinted to read it. It was just the very edge of a handwritten note with just the endings of a few words.

    ...*ull*
    ...*ick*
    ...*son*

"Those endings could go with lots of words," Millie said. "I want a copy of that. Can you text it to me?"

"Me too," I said.

Seth looked uncertain.

"There's an apple pie in it for you if you text it to me." Millie turned to me. "I'll text it to you after."

Seth sighed. "I suppose it won't do any harm."

"Good," Millie said. "Now, until we figure out what that note really says, we have a lot of clues that point to Tony Murano. How many clues do you have that point to Josie?"

Seth opened his mouth but I cut in. "Never mind, don't answer that. This is what we have on Tony. His shoe print was under the window, Tony has a bad temper and Charles wrote a bad review about his lemon meringue pie."

Mom nodded. "Why would Tony's print be outside

the window if he wasn't climbing out and why would he be climbing out if he didn't kill Charles?"

"Maybe the print wasn't from Tony," Seth said. "I don't think you can tell for sure that print was from his shoe. And besides, it's risky to go out of the window. And how did he get in and mess with the stairs without anyone noticing? It makes more sense that it was an inside job."

"No one inside the guesthouse has a motive...Well, except maybe Tina." Mom turned to me. "Didn't Ava say she saw Tina sneaking out of Charles's room?"

I glanced at Seth. He didn't look surprised. Could he have known about Tina and Charles's affair already? Maybe I wasn't giving him enough credit. "She did. And Stella Dumont saw her down at the sleazy motel."

"Maybe Tina and Tony were in on it together," Mom said.

Millie bit her bottom lip. "You know, now that you mention it, didn't we notice that Tina works for the culinary section of the paper? Is it possible she and Tony know each other?"

Mom slapped her forehead. "Of course! That's it. This wasn't about a bad review at all—Seth was right about that. It was about a love triangle."

"Love triangle?" Seth looked more confused than ever.

"Yes!" Mom said. "What if Tina was having an affair with both Charles and Tony? Tony found out and came here and murdered Charles out of jealousy!"

"That would explain why Tina was checking into that other motel. Maybe Stella really did see her. She didn't want Charles to know she was having an affair with Tony," I said.

"That makes perfect sense," Millie said. "And Tony would have to go to a hotel because his wife seems very jealous. Did you see the way she acted in the kitchen?"

I nodded vigorously. "And she also seemed suspicious of him. Like she suspected he was having an affair."

"That's it then." Millie turned to Seth. "Are you going to make an arrest?"

"That's not really solid evidence," he said. "We like to have a few clues other than people's say-so. Especially when your say-so is tainted."

"Tainted? How?" Millie was indignant.

"You guys are trying to get Josie off the suspect list," Seth said.

"We are not!" Mom said. "Well, I mean, we are, but that's 'cause Josie isn't guilty."

"Seth Chamberlain, you know these clues are good clues. This is a good working theory. Are you going to check it out or do you want me to never cook you a batch of snickerdoodles again?" Millie asked.

Seth's lips quirked in a smile and his eyes twinkled. "Fine. I'll check them out. I suppose I could find out where they were the night of Charles's death and see how well this Tina person knew him. But don't expect anything to come of it."

Chapter Thirteen

Flora hadn't washed the dishes I left in the sink, so after Mom and Millie left, I got to work on those. Nero and Marlowe accompanied me to the kitchen and stood meowing at their food bowls. Nero looked like he was getting a little fat, but I still fed them some kibble.

I thought about the clues as I worked. The sound of Mike's hammering three floors up was comforting. Even the cats' meows and little crunches as they ate the kibble made me feel at home.

I should probably move their dishes out of the kitchen, just in case Barbara Littlefield made an appearance. Actually, one good thing about having a murder at the guesthouse was that it seemed to be keeping her away. She wasn't due to come and inspect anything until Mike was done with that room next week. I could move the cat bowls before then.

From my spot at the kitchen sink I could see the Smugglers Bay Inn below the dark storm clouds that had rolled in. This time there were no seagulls around. That must make Stella happy. Thinking of her made me realize I had really been hoping that she was the killer. Though Tony Murano did seem more like the type, I still had to wonder why Stella had been lurking around the guesthouse. Was she really here to see Mike? And if Tony was the killer, was he in cahoots with Tina? The thought of having an accomplice to murder right under my roof turned my blood cold.

I contemplated asking Tina some leading questions that might trip her up so that she inadvertently confessed, but then realized maybe that wasn't very smart considering she might be a killer. The advancing storm would be a great backdrop for her to murder me. The sound of thunder could mask the bludgeoning. Maybe I'd better not. Besides, though her little black convertible was parked in the lot, I hadn't seen her all afternoon so assumed she must be ensconced in her room.

Just before I finished the dishes, Ava Grantham popped her head into the kitchen.

"Oh, hi, Josie, I was wondering if I could get some tea. This damp weather is getting into my old bones." She wrung her hands together.

"Of course, why don't you sit in the front parlor and I'll bring some out."

She nodded gratefully and headed off toward the front parlor while I boiled water, got out a selection of teabags and threw some pumpkin muffins into a basket with the butter.

Ava sat in the overstuffed chair looking out the window at the storm. She looked up when I entered. "I hope the storm passes over quickly."

It was almost dark and the churning sea had a rough, ominous feel. Great ambience for a murder, I thought, but refrained from saying so. The last thing I needed was another one of those.

"Hopefully it won't be too bad." I put the tea and basket down in front of her.

"Oh, you brought muffins! How lovely."

The thought struck me that Ava had seemed to know an awful lot about what had gone on between Tina and Charles. Since I couldn't really ask Tina, maybe Ava would have some insight. I picked out a muffin and buttered it while Ava sipped her tea.

"Has there been any news on the murder case?" Ava asked the question casually. Perhaps a little bit too casually? I looked up to see a glimmer of interest in her eye.

"The police are still looking into it, but I may have found a little clue." I wasn't going to tell Ava what I'd discovered, but I wanted to feel her out and see how willing she would be to talk.

"Oh, really?" Ava watched me over the rose dotted rim of her china teacup.

"Well, I don't know much, but I heard it might have something to do with a jealous lover. And you said you saw Tina..." I let my voice trail off.

"Oh, yes I did." Ava nodded. "Tina and Charles."

"And Charles was the type to fool around, you say?"

"Certainly. I'd seen it happen many, many times. But who would be jealous?" She paused and then her eyes widened. "Oh? You think Charles had another lover and Tina killed him because she was jealous?"

Actually I hadn't thought of it that way. But what if Ava was right? What if I had it backward and the jealous lover wasn't someone who was mad that Charles was fooling around with their woman, but rather someone who was angry that Charles was fooling around on them?

"Or Tina had a lover that killed Charles. I guess either way, jealousy is a strong motivator," I said.

Ava nodded her head enthusiastically. "Yes, that is a very good theory. Are the police going to make an arrest?"

"That I don't know," I said.

Ava nibbled on a muffin and made a face. "Now that would be one for the columns. A love-triangle murder."

I frowned. Hopefully Ava wasn't considering publishing a story about Charles's murder.

"Such a sad thing that people want to hear about murders and affairs now instead of balls and coming-out parties like in my day," Ava said.

"People certainly have become ghoulish," I agreed.

Ava brushed the crumbs off her fingers and stood. "Well, I guess things never stay the same. I'm just glad the police are onto somebody. I hate to think of the killer just wandering around in here. Now that the tea has warmed me up, I think I'll get my old bones under the comforters. Always get so tired once the sun goes down." She glanced out the window and then headed toward the front stairs.

She must've passed Flora because I heard her asking the maid to bring her an extra blanket. To my surprise Flora agreed and said she would be there in a few minutes. With the lack of work Flora did, I figured she would've told Ava she was clocking out, but she hadn't. Maybe Flora wasn't a total loss after all.

Flora came into the parlor and flopped down in the chair Ava had just vacated. "Dang guests got me running all around." She glanced at the basket. "Oh, muffins, don't mind if I do."

She plucked a muffin out and popped half of it into

her mouth. "I'm exhausted. Making all those beds is hard work and I also did some dusting and now I've got to get that blanket. You know the dusting is hard enough, even without all that cat hair." Her words were barely intelligible because she was mumbling around her food.

Suddenly I realized that as Flora made the beds, she would know if Tina had been home the night Charles was killed.

"It must be very difficult," I agreed, pushing the muffin basket closer since she'd already finished the one she'd started. "You must be glad you don't have to make them all every day."

She swallowed hard and frowned at me. "What are you getting at? Are you saying I don't do my job every day?"

"No, not at all. Just that if the beds haven't been slept in…"

"Yeah, that's right. Why would I have to make the bed if it hadn't been slept in? Did that little tart Tina complain? I don't see any reason to make her bed if it wasn't slept in. Well, I'll tell you, she's a fine one sneaking off to another hotel." She leaned back in her chair.

"So Tina wasn't here one night?"

"No. And I'll have you know there's no sense in making the bed if someone isn't here. It's bad enough I have to clean up straw and feathers and muck."

"Straw?"

"Yes, those old people with the cameras. When I went in to clean up their room it was dirty with straw and twigs and feathers. Pigs!"

Nero and Marlowe had come into the room and jumped up on my lap. I absently petted them as I thought about Flora's words. Straw, twigs, and feathers sounded like nesting material. I knew they were bird-watchers but I had no idea they'd gotten close enough to the nests to have nesting material on them.

Thunder boomed in the distance and Flora jumped up.

"Looks like the storm's brewing and I aim to get home before the big rain starts." She pointed at her owlish eyes. "Can't see very good with these old peepers anymore. I'll just get that blanket to the old lady and be on my way."

"Okay, don't worry about me, I'll clean up in here." As if she would worry. The first raindrops splattered on the window, but I wasn't paying attention to the weather. I was busy wondering what the Weatherbys had been up to and whether or not Seth Chamberlain had confronted Tony Murano.

*

Nero practically jumped out of his fur as thunder boomed in the distance. He snuggled further into Josie's lap, enjoying the soft stroking of her fingers more than he cared to admit.

Marlowe kneaded Josie's thigh. "I don't like where this is going. Josie might be getting herself into a heap of trouble. She was asking Ava a lot of questions about Tina and Charles. She might be getting ready to interrogate a suspect."

"Let's just hope she doesn't confront the wrong person." Nero glanced at the basket of muffins. He wasn't much of a muffin eater, but the butter, on the other hand, was quite delectable and enticing.

"You think she'll notice if we lick the butter?" Marlowe echoed his thoughts.

"Most likely." Nero glanced longingly at the bright yellow stick in the crystal dish. "I think we need to focus our attentions on making sure Josie doesn't do anything rash."

"Yeah. Especially if the killer is around on a night like this." Marlowe shivered and glanced out the window.

"Maybe we should sleep in the bed with her tonight?" Nero tried to keep from quaking as another thunderclap boomed. "I mean for her comfort, of course, not for ours."

"We can try."

"Though, of course, you know what we must do," Nero said.

"Of course. Try to sleep on her head and then only after she has shoved us away twenty-five times can we curl up beside her, but we must take up a sizable amount of space on the bed." Marlowe repeated what Nero had instructed her of early on.

Nero nodded. "You have learned much."

Josie set Nero aside and he hissed at her to indicate that she should only do that when he wanted her to. She looked down at him. "When we were just getting along, now you hiss at me?"

Nero purred and put his head down and she patted him.

"Now that's better. I suppose I better figure out what to make for breakfast tomorrow."

Nero and Marlowe followed Josie into the kitchen and watched as she fussed around with the recipes.

"We must stick to her like glue, she's headstrong and may say the wrong thing to the wrong person," Nero said.

"Agreed," Marlowe said.

Nero glanced out at the dark night, a grim feeling of foreboding coming over him. "And tonight especially, we must be alert. My seventh sense is telling me the killer may return to the scene of the crime, and, if he does, we will have to be here to protect our human."

Chapter Fourteen

I listened to the rain splatter against the windows and prayed the power wouldn't go out while I pawed through the recipe file in search of something to make for breakfast the next morning. The sour-cream coffee cake would be nice, a great comforting treat after a big stormy night. Where was the recipe? Maybe it had gotten wedged somewhere when I dropped the file the other day. The cabinet door under the sink didn't close right. Maybe it had fluttered inside and was lying among the bottles of Windex and stacks of sponges.

I got down on all fours and stuck my head inside the cabinet. Marlowe and Nero trotted up beside me. In fact, they'd been sticking to me like glue all night. Probably afraid of the storm.

Kaboom!

The cats jumped and so did I, hitting my head on the inside of the cabinet. Ouch. At least the sound of the thunder had been muted with my head inside that thing.

I pulled out my head. I was expecting to hear a flurry of footsteps above as my guests leapt out of bed. But no. They all must have Ambien prescriptions because they were apparently fast asleep, tucked into their quilt-covered beds.

I stood, rubbing the back of my head, and Nero jumped on the counter.

Meow.

"Hey, I just washed that. Get down." I waved my hands at the cat, who simply turned his back on me to look out the window. Good thing Barbara Littlefield wouldn't be making a surprise visit tonight in the storm.

I followed his gaze out the window just in time to see a bolt of lightning illuminate the turbulent surf in the cove near the Smugglers Bay Inn. No seagulls were flying around in this storm.

Meroow!

Marlowe paced over by the door to the hallway. The sound of her meow reminded me of the tone of her wailing when we found Charles's body. Hopefully it wasn't a tone reserved only for body finding.

Nero leaped down from the counter and trotted toward the door, looking over his shoulder at me.

Kaboom!

The thunder sure was loud.

Creak.

Wait, what was that? One of the guests? I tilted my head to the side and cocked my ear toward the ceiling. No, the creaking hadn't come from upstairs, it had come from the direction of the foyer. Both cats were now sitting in the doorway that led to the hallway and looking at me expectantly. Were they trying to alert me to an intruder?

I grabbed the first weapon I could find. A rolling pin. Not the new glass kind. The heavy old-fashioned wooden kind.

My heart pounded against my rib cage as I crept out into the darkened hallway.

Creak.

Whoever it was, they were near the stairs! Was that the killer coming back to the scene of the crime? And if so, why?

I probably should've called the cops, but I didn't want to alert the intruder to the fact that I knew he was there. Now I had the element of surprise I didn't want to lose it. If I took my phone out and called, they might hear me and run off. I needed to catch him in the act and then hopefully detain him long enough for the police to come.

I moved slowly along the hallway, my rolling pin raised above my head.

A big hulking shadow loomed by the stairs. He looked like he was about to head down the hallway that led to the west wing. Just as I suspected, the killer was returning, probably to make sure he hadn't left some sort of clue.

I was almost upon him when lightning lit the hallway, exposing the intruder. My heart crashed along with the accompanying sound of thunder.

It was Tony Murano and he was holding something shiny in his hand.

I must have made a noise because Tony spun around.

I flicked on the lights and raised the rolling pin over my head. "You! Put that down. I knew you were the killer!"

Tony shoved his hand behind his back, scrunched up his face and shaded his eyes against the light with his free hand. "Huh? Listen, lady, you've caused enough trouble for me."

He took a step toward me. I couldn't see what was in his left hand. Was it the cleaver I'd seen him wielding in the restaurant? He seemed to enjoy hacking things with it. But I wasn't going to let him intimidate me. "That's far enough, Tony. I've already called the police and they'll be here any minute."

"Good, because you should be arrested."

"Me? You're the killer!"

"No. You are. The *marriage* killer. What do you mean coming over to my restaurant and getting my wife all upset. You should mind your own business."

Huh? This wasn't going the way I thought it would. Why was he talking about his wife? Perhaps he was trying to distract me.

"I'm not falling for that! You broke in here! I bet you think we're getting too close to the truth and want to make sure you didn't leave more than just a footprint at the scene of the crime."

"I didn't break in." Tony gestured toward the door. "I was knocking on the door but nobody answered. It was unlocked so I just came in. It was dark in here and I was standing, getting my bearings, when you came out and tried to attack me."

I looked at the door. Had I left it unlocked? I couldn't remember, but surely I would've heard him knocking? Then again, I'd had my head inside the cabinet and barely heard the thunder.

Nero and Marlowe were pacing around Tony with their tails high in the air. Now, what exactly did that mean? I was sure they were trying to tell me something, but was it that Tony was the killer or that he was not the killer? Either way, I wasn't safe with him in here. I dug in my pocket for my cell phone and quickly realized I'd left it in the kitchen. Now what? Maybe one of the guests would come down and help distract him, and I could clonk him over the head with the rolling pin.

My arm was getting really tired, but I raised the rolling pin higher. "You can't talk your way out of this. I know that you snuck over the other night and killed Charles. Maybe you broke in the same way you did tonight. And you went out the window afterward."

"Charles? Who is Charles and why would I kill him?"

"Charles Prescott. The Laughing Gourmet. He wrote a bad review of your restaurant last year and when you found out he was staying here, you took your revenge."

"Bad review? You mean that review on my lemon meringue pie?" Tony laughed, the sinister sound echoing along the hallway. "Why would I kill him over that? That review was good for business."

"You expect me to believe a bad review is good for business?"

"Sure, that review was just sour grapes and it hasn't hurt me none. In fact, it's brought more people to my restaurant asking for the sour lemon meringue pie. Turns out there's a whole bunch of people who like their pie sour," Tony said. "So you see, I wouldn't want to kill him. I'd want to thank him."

I gnawed my bottom lip. It seemed like Tony might

be telling the truth about that. Maybe my mom had been right about the love triangle. "All right, maybe that review was not the reason why you killed him. Maybe you killed Charles Prescott because of the love triangle!"

The stairs creaked and we looked up to see Tina standing there, her eyes wide, her mouth hanging open as she stared at Tony. "You killed Charles?"

Tony's brow furrowed. "What? No. I didn't kill him. I wasn't mad about that review."

"Not the review," I said. "You were jealous because you had to share Tina with him!"

Tina gasped. Tony's gaze jerked to Tina's face. He looked like he was ready to cry. "You were having an affair with this Charles guy?"

Tina's eyes were about as big as Flora's. "No. I swear!" She rushed down the stairs to Tony's side. "You're the only one I'm having an affair with."

Tony looked dubious. He turned to me. "What do you know about this affair?"

I crossed my arms over my chest, mostly because my right arm was aching from holding up the rolling pin. "One of our other guests saw Tina sneaking out of Charles's room."

Tony looked at Tina, crestfallen. "Is that true? You were cheating on me?"

Tina glared at me. "No, it is not true. Well, it's partly true. I *was* in Charles's room."

"Aha!" I said.

Meow. The cats obviously agreed.

"But not because I was having an affair with him," Tina added.

Tony still looked dubious. "Why were you in there then?"

Now that his attention was on Tina, I thought it might be a good time to do something to detain him for the police. I needed to know what he had for a weapon first. I tried to peek behind his back, but all I saw was what looked like a plastic bag. Had he brought the cleaver in a bag? I supposed it would raise suspicion if he walked around holding it in his hand.

Tina sighed and looked down at the floor. She shuffled her feet, then she said, "I was in his room looking for his recipe book."

"Aha!" I said again. My vocabulary had apparently diminished during the conversation.

"A recipe book." Tony looked like he wanted to believe her but wasn't sure.

"Charles was supposed to be writing a book with unique recipes. It was going to be a hit. And...well...my food column isn't going very well and I just thought if I got a peek at the recipes maybe I could recreate some and write a book too." She whipped out a tissue and sniffled, tears welling up in her big blue eyes. I could tell by the look on Tony's face that the tears had softened him.

"Wait a minute, so you're the one who took his cookbook?" I asked.

Tina nodded, dabbing her eyes with the tissue. "It's in my room. But I swear he wasn't here when I did it. I had seen him that night up on the cliffs and I knew it would be a long time before he could make it back, so I figured that was my chance to get in his room and look for it."

"Let me get this straight. You weren't mad about the lemon meringue pie review, the two of you are having an affair, but Tina wasn't also having an affair with Charles?"

They both glanced at each other and nodded. That explained why Tony's wife was acting like he was a cheater. He was. But was he a killer too? If Tina wasn't having an affair with Charles, then there would be no motive for Tony to kill him. And her affair with Tony could also explain why Stella had seen Tina out at the Timber Me Motel.

"Did you guys meet at the Timber Me Motel?"

Tony's eyes widened. "Yeah, how do you know about that?"

"I have my sources." I turned to Tina. "But you weren't having an affair with Charles?"

She shook her head.

"And you were seen coming out of his room because you stole the cookbook?"

She nodded vigorously. "Yeah, and I can prove it too. It's in my room upstairs. I'll get it."

Before either of us could answer, she ran up the stairs.

I turned to Tony. There were still unanswered questions, not the least of which was why he'd snuck in here carrying a weapon in a bag. "Well then, if you and Tina had your affair at the Timber Me Motel, why did you sneak out the window in the west wing?"

His eyes widened. "How did you know I did that? Do you have cameras in this place? Do you have cameras in the rooms? You watching what's going on?"

"No. We saw a footprint in the bark mulch outside the very room Charles Prescott was killed in." I glanced down at his feet. "It was a chef's clog and the sides had extensive wear on them, as if the owner walked on the sides of his feet."

Tony backed up. I was a little nervous because he was still holding his left hand behind him. What did he have back there? "I didn't kill Charles. But I did sneak out that window. I came here one night to meet Tina when she first arrived in town. But then that busybody old lady saw us. I panicked and wanted to get out without being seen. I was afraid word would get back to my wife. Tina knew that section of the guesthouse was closed off so we went down there and I went out the window."

"What night was that?"

"It must've been two nights before the guy was offed. Because after getting caught out in the hall here, we decided to lay low the next day and meet at the sleazy motel on Tuesday and that's where we were the night that guy died."

I cringed at his coarse language, but that wasn't the worst thing about what he'd said. If he really was at the sleazy motel the night Charles was killed, then he might have an alibi. And if he did, then who was the killer?

Tina was in the breakfast room the next morning, though, so did that mean he might be lying about having been at the Timber Me Motel? Then again, I didn't know if she'd come into the dining room from her room or from outside. It was possible she'd just gotten in from her midnight interlude or had snuck back in the wee hours of the morning. If they were trying to fly under the radar, that would make sense.

Tony must've seen the look of doubt on my face because he continued, "You can ask that sheriff guy. In fact, he came to visit me after you got poking your nose into my business. That's how I know when this Charles guy was killed. That sheriff started spouting off some stuff about me being a suspect and I told him just what I told you. He went down to the sleazy motel to verify my alibi. And that's why I came here tonight. I knew I had to explain myself and beg you not to tell my wife."

Before I could answer, Tina came back down the stairs with the cookbook. It was a blue three-ring binder just like Ava had described.

"See? This is what I got from Charles's room." She looked down at the floor again. "I know it was wrong to steal it. And after he died, I tried to put it back, but the police were in there and then you were in there and, well, I figured since he was dead maybe I could use it…"

I opened the book. It was filled with handwritten recipes. I turned to Tony. "If all this is true and you only came here to talk to me, then why did you bring the cleaver?"

"Cleaver?" Tony looked down at his hand. "Oh, this?" He whipped his other hand out from behind his back, the white plastic bag dangling menacingly. "This isn't a cleaver."

I stepped back as he reached into the bag.

"It's a ricotta pie. I brought it as a peace offering. I was hoping that if I got in your good graces you and those crazy old ladies would stop coming to the restaurant and wouldn't tell my wife about the affair with Tina."

And just like that, my prime suspect evaporated. If what Tony said was true, I could easily verify his alibi with Seth. And why would he lie about it?

I accepted the ricotta pie, grimaced as Tina and Tony gave each other a sickening smooch goodbye and then proceeded to the kitchen. At least I had the ricotta pie to offer my guests for breakfast. I didn't have time to sort through recipes and put something together for the morning. I needed to come up with a new suspect.

*

I put the ricotta pie away and went to my suite to settle in with the cats. Okay, I admit I did take a teeny sliver of pie with me, but only because I had to test it out to see if it was good enough for the guests. Tina had gone back to bed and by some miracle the rest of the guesthouse had not been awakened by the argument down in the foyer, so it was nice and quiet.

The owner's suite wasn't big, but it was comfortable and cozy. It consisted of a small fireplace, a living room that had a window overlooking the ocean, complete with blue cushioned window seat, a bedroom that was part of the rounded turret, and a small bath. It was done in neutral shades of gray and mocha.

The trendy colors blended nicely with the antique touches, like the carved mantel and the hardwood flooring, to give it an eclectic feel. The living room had a microsuede sectional and I settled in, pulling a fleece blanket over me. The cats immediately jumped on the blanket and curled up beside me. The low hum of their purrs was comforting. Maybe I could get used to having cat companions.

I sipped my chamomile tea and dug into the ricotta pie. It was creamy and sweet. If I hadn't been married to a chef, I would have been grossed out by the idea of ricotta pie. I mean, wasn't that something you put in a lasagna? But I'd had it before and Tony's was much better than Clive's.

As I savored the pie, I flipped through the recipe book. Charles was making a book of recipes that included berries. He even had a section of information about each berry. There were berry tarts, berry pies, berry dressings, even berry bread. There were even flockenberries in there. Maybe that was why he'd been on the cliff, to research the flockenberries.

I closed the book and sighed. "Well, I guess these berries probably didn't have anything to do with Charles's death."

Meow.

Nero hopped down from the sofa and trotted over to the old mahogany writing desk Millie had left for me, casting a glance back at Marlowe, who soon joined him.

"Yeah, I know. Dead end, right?" I said. "Who would kill someone over berries?"

Nero jumped up on the desk and batted at a pen.

"Unfortunately, now I'm back to square one."

Merope. The pen clattered onto the wood floor.

"Hey, cut that out."

Nero stared at me with his golden eyes as he pushed another pen off.

"You're doing that on purpose!"

Mew. Purr.

He pushed another pen.

"Okay, now I'm getting angry." I disentangled myself from my fuzzy cocoon, picked up the pens and put them back on the desk. Marlowe was sitting in the window seat and I patted the top of her head.

"At least you're a good girl, not tossing things off the desk." I gave Nero a pointed look.

Nero narrowed his gaze. *Mew.*

I kept petting Marlowe, who was gazing out the window toward the Smugglers Bay Inn. It had stopped raining and the silver light of the moon highlighted the edges of the clouds and bounced off the rolling surf. Marlowe was probably thinking about getting out and catching some midnight mice.

"Not tonight, my friend."

Merow.

The tone of her voice indicated she wasn't very happy with that, but I was the boss.

Mreep!

Nero swatted a small pad of notepaper off the desk. Was he jealous that I was paying so much attention to Marlowe?

Meow!

Marlowe leapt off the window seat and lunged for the paper, tearing it with her claws.

Meroo!

Nero jumped down and swatted at it, shredding a few pieces off the pad.

Marlowe pounced, Nero swatted, pieces of paper flew.

"Hey, hey!" I intercepted the notebook as it slid across the floor and picked it up.

Both cats screeched to a stop and looked up, innocent expressions plastered on their furry faces.

I looked down at the paper, which was practically shredded into confetti. "Boy, you guys have sharp claws."

It was only a cheap notepad, but I'd started writing a grocery list and now you could only see the last few letters of the words. Now what was the food that ended in "ery" that I'd wanted? Celery? What other words ended in that? This was like the partial note that had been found in Charles's room that the police had assumed was the review he'd been killed for. I'd assumed Charles had been killed because of a review too and that turned out to be wrong. If my assumptions about the motive behind Charles's death were wrong, then maybe that partial piece of paper wasn't a review after all.

I rushed to my phone to look at the picture of the note Millie had texted to me.

. . . *ull*
. . . *ick*
. . . *son*

What if "ull" was for *gull*? The gulls were *sick*. Was it possible the letter had something to do with the reason for that? That last word ended in "son." Poison? *Gull, sick, poison.* Charles had been seen on the cliffs. What if he'd stumbled upon some evidence pertaining to what was happening to the gulls? And what if he knew who was behind it? Ava had mentioned that Charles wasn't a nice man; he wasn't beyond throwing someone under the bus or lying or cheating. And he needed money.

What if the note was a blackmail note? Someone being blackmailed would have a much deeper motivation to kill Charles than someone he was writing a bad review about.

But if this was a blackmail note, and if the note really was the reason Charles was murdered, then who was he blackmailing and what did he have on them?

Chapter Fifteen

The next morning, I arranged the slices of ricotta pie on a fancy plate so that no one would realize I'd taken a slice out the night before. With only four people at the guesthouse, there was plenty of pie, and I wanted it to look nice on the buffet. But one can't have only pie for breakfast, so I also got out some eggs and bacon. I was cracking the eggs when Mom and Millie burst through the kitchen door.

"Josie! Bad news! Seth Chamberlain informed me that Tony Murano can't be the killer. He has an alibi." Millie pushed me aside and took over egg duty. Fine by me, I didn't really want to scramble them anyway and besides, I was bursting to tell them about my visit from Tony and my new suspicions about why Charles was killed.

As if summoned by Millie's voice, Nero and Marlowe trotted into the kitchen and sat at her feet, gazing up at her.

"I know. And there's more." I moved to the bacon, which was crackling and sizzling. The cats swerved their gaze in my direction. I removed the fully cooked pieces and put them on a paper towel to drain, then added a few more slabs to the pan.

Millie turned to look at me. "Do tell."

I told them about my visit from Tony and how Tina hadn't been having an affair with Charles, but had been in his room to take the cookbook.

"Hmmm, well, that is a bummer." Millie opened the spice drawer and started fishing around. "Where's the vanilla? It's a secret ingredient for the eggs."

"Should be in there." I peered in and spied it way in the back. "There it is."

"So now what?" Mom had helped herself to a piece of ricotta pie and was sitting at the table. "Seems like we have to start from square one with the suspects."

"Not necessarily," I said. "I think we might have been barking up the wrong tree with the review angle anyway."

Millie poured the eggs into the pan and started mixing them around while I told them about my suspicions that the note was really a blackmail letter concerning the gulls.

"You don't say?" Mom glanced toward the cove. "Do you think someone is harming the gulls on purpose?"

"Maybe. Charles was seen on the cliff and that's where they nest. He might have discovered someone doing something to their nests." I lowered my voice. "I already have some suspects."

"Who?" Millie rummaged for serving dishes and then started spooning the eggs into a silver bowl with a lid.

"Well, now let's think of this logically," Mom said, her forkful of ricotta pie hovering near her lips. "The partial note was found in Charles's room, which seems to indicate the killer was in his room. So who visited Charles?"

I thought about that for a second as I layered the

crispy bacon onto a white ironstone platter. "I don't think anyone came to visit him. At least no one that I saw."

"Ava Grantham said she saw Tina in his room," Millie pointed out.

"But Tina was there because she was stealing the cookbook. Charles wasn't even at the guesthouse then, because she'd seen him on the cliff." I picked a piece of bacon out of the pile and crunched. "He could have written the letter earlier, maybe he confronted the person and they tore it up and Charles took part of it back with him."

"But the killer had to have been in the guesthouse at some point, either the night they killed Charles or when they sabotaged the stairs. And no one saw anyone who wasn't supposed to be here," Millie said. "With Josie, Flora, and Mike around I would think someone would have seen something."

"Charles was killed in the middle of the night; everyone was asleep." Mom snagged a piece of bacon and broke off two tiny morsels, then tossed one to Marlowe and one to Nero.

"Not too much of that, Rose," Millie admonished. "That's not good for them. I hope you aren't going to get in the habit of feeding junk to the cats like your mother does, Josie."

"Huh?" I hadn't been paying attention because my brain was still processing the fact that no one had seen anyone in the guesthouse who wasn't supposed to be there. "What if none of us saw an intruder in the guesthouse because the killer is one of the guests?"

"Who?"

I glanced around to make sure none of the guests were hovering in the hallway. Especially not the guests that were now on my suspect list. The hall was empty.

"The Weatherbys," I whispered. "They are very interested in the gulls and Flora found straw and feathers in their room. Tina said she saw them up on the cliffs near the nests!"

"Well, of course she did." Millie looked at me as if I was batty. "They are birdwatchers. I mean, surely you've seen them with all their cameras and binoculars."

"Oh, I've seen them all right. But the other day, Mike asked Ron some questions about his camera and Mike said that the answers seemed to indicate that Ron didn't know much about the camera. Now wouldn't he be somewhat of an expert if he was a birdwatcher?" I asked.

Mom pressed her lips together. "Maybe. But you know us older folks aren't that good with technology. I had to ask your brother to help me with my new smartphone."

Millie nodded. "She's right. And they hardly seem like the type to bludgeon someone and try to make it look like he fell down the stairs."

"Right, someone would have to have carpentry skills for that," Mom added.

"Either that or maybe they thought an elderly small-town sheriff wouldn't be able to figure out the scene was tampered with. I remember Ron made a comment about small-town police forces not doing a thorough job. Maybe he was banking on that," I said.

Millie and Mom's brows drew sharply together.

"Did you say elderly? Seth is our age," Mom said.

"Err...I meant senior."

"Right, well anyway." Millie picked up the serving bowls. "It's time to serve the breakfast. Meanwhile we need to figure out exactly what the Weatherbys have been up to."

"How do we do that?" Mom picked up the plate with the ricotta pie on it, eyeing the pieces as if she was counting them to make sure she'd get leftovers.

"We ask who saw them around and what exactly they were doing. Were they watching the gulls or doing something more? That sort of thing," Millie said.

"What about Barbara Littlefield?" Mom asked. "She's always up on the cliff mothering that lousewort. If the Weatherbys have been up to some shenanigans, chances are she's seen them. I'd say someone should talk to her."

I grabbed the pitcher of juice from the fridge and followed Millie to the dining room. Mom had a point about Barbara. Maybe the crotchety building inspector would have her uses after all.

Chapter Sixteen

Millie and Mom had cast suspicious glances at the Weatherbys all during breakfast. It was a wonder they didn't catch on to the fact that we suspected them. I couldn't help but study them myself for suspicious activity, but they acted normally. Tina, on the other hand, kept staring at me, then averting her eyes, then dropping things on the floor. Clearly she was nervous that I'd tell everyone about her affair with Tony. I wouldn't. That was the least of my worries.

Ava seemed oblivious to all of it and enjoyed two slices of ricotta pie while sipping tea from her dainty china teacup and chatting with Millie and Mom.

After breakfast, Mom and Millie helped me clean up and I drew the short straw so it was determined I would talk to Barbara. That's how I found myself standing outside Barbara's office in the town hall with the last piece of ricotta pie in a handy reusable plastic container.

The door to Barbara's office was a giant imposing oak door. I wouldn't have been surprised if it had had a humongous metal doorknocker and squeaky iron hinges, but it was just a regular oak four-panel door.

"Go ahead and knock, she's not busy," the receptionist prompted because I was hesitating. "She doesn't bite."

I sucked in a breath wondering how badly I wanted to find out if she knew about the Weatherbys doing anything strange on the cliff. I reminded myself that Sheriff Chamberlain still thought I could be involved and tapped on the door.

"What do you want?" Her voice bellowed through the door and it didn't sound friendly.

"Umm . . . It's Josie Waters. I brought you some pie."

"Oh, good. Come on in, I can serve you this fine in person."

Great. I opened the door anyway. I figured she'd give me the fine no matter what, but maybe the pie would butter her up a bit. At the very least I still needed to ask about the Weatherbys.

I don't know what I had expected her office to look like. Probably sparse and unwelcoming and filled with stainless-steel furniture, bland indoor-outdoor carpet and uncomfortable plastic chairs. But what was inside was something else entirely. It looked like a tropical paradise.

Lush green plants lined the windowsills, crowded the tables and obscured the desk. There were plants of every size. From tall palm-like plants that stood in giant pots in the corner, to tiny seedlings under a fluorescent lamp. The heat was turned up to sweltering.

"Well, well, well. I didn't expect or want to see you, but I guess it is convenient." Barbara's voice came from somewhere in front of me, but all I could see were plants. Then, two claw-like hands reached out to part the leaves of a gaggle of giant philodendrons that sat on the desk, and Barbara's face peeked through, her eyes narrowed, mouth twisted in a sour puss.

"Hi, Barb—I mean Mrs. Littlefield!" I tried to act cheery and shoved the pie out in front of me. "I had this left over from breakfast and Millie thought it would be nice to bring it down."

I heard a chair push back and I assumed she had stood. I couldn't tell because the plants were so tall. She appeared around the corner of the desk (yes, it was dull gray metal just as I'd envisioned).

"Millie Sullivan, you say?" She eyed the pie with suspicion and I hoped she wouldn't recognize it as Tony's. Was it bad etiquette to re-gift pie?

I nodded and handed it over. Barbara grabbed it and found some space on the desk for it, then folded her arms across her chest. "That wouldn't be a bribe now, would it?"

"What? No, of course not."

"I don't take bribes." She shoved a piece of paper in my hand. "This here's your fine for having a corpse on the premises during breakfast."

"That's a real thing you can get fined for?" I stared at the paper, my palms starting to sweat. I wasn't sure if the sweating was because of the two-hundred-and-fifty-dollar price tag or the fact that the room was sweltering. Two hundred and fifty dollars? I could barely come up with that, but I knew it was no use to argue with her. Better not to anger her either; I still had a lot of renovations I had to get her approval for.

Barbara didn't seem affected by the heat. "Yes, it's a real thing and payable within thirty days. You better get your act together over there or you might find yourself without a guesthouse to run."

I swallowed hard, sweat beaded on my forehead. I felt like a chastised schoolgirl. "Yes, ma'am."

"Okay, now get lost."

Shoot. I had to ask her about the cliffs. I wiped sweat out of my eyes and glanced at the plants. Inspiration struck. The best way to get people to like you was to talk about something they were interested in. Barbara was certainly interested in plants. "I see you have some nice plants here. They look so healthy."

She turned and frowned at me. "What's it to you?"

"Nothing. Just, um... they look nice."

"Thanks." She blinked and I thought I saw her eyes soften, but then they grew cold and hard just as quickly.

This wasn't working out the way I'd hoped. Okay, be more specific and get her talking. I walked over to the plants that were growing under the lights and made a pretense of admiring them while sweat rolled down my back. There were some dead plants on the lower shelf and I purposely didn't mention those, focusing on the live ones instead. "Take these for example, they're very green even though they are so young." I bent closer to them and reached out my hand to touch one.

"Watch out!" Barbara rushed over and practically slapped my hand away. "Those are endangered lousewort. Be careful."

Bingo! The perfect opening for me to ask about the cliff. "Speaking of that. I've heard some of my guests talking about the lousewort and was wondering if you've seen them on the cliffs?"

"Your guests? No. That area is off limits."

"I know, but it has a nice view."

"View, schmoo. The endangered plants are up there and no one is allowed."

"But the Weatherbys are avid birdwatchers and the gulls' nests are near there and they eat the berries. Surely you must have seen them up there?"

She just glared at me and repeated, "No one goes up there."

Darn. She hadn't seen anything. She'd probably have made a big scene about it if she had seen them anyway. Was it possible that I was on the wrong track, that Charles and the Weatherbys weren't up there? "Not even Charles Prescott?"

"You mean the man who died?"

I nodded.

"Nope. Never even met the man, much less saw him in a protected area. I would have written him up if I had. Now if you're done asking me inane questions and trying to bribe me, I have work to do." She practically shoved me out the door.

I supposed that Charles could have been on the cliff when Barbara wasn't there. She spent a lot of time tending to the lousewort, but she couldn't possibly be up there every minute. And if the Weatherbys were up to something suspicious, wouldn't they make sure they were alone? Unfortunately my whole trip had been a waste, but just because Barbara hadn't seen anyone didn't mean that they hadn't been there.

*

Barbara hadn't been a wealth of information; I left her office disappointed. I had been hoping she could corroborate my theory about the Weatherbys and had seen them doing something suspicious.

Since I was in town, I figured it was only fitting that I pop in and visit Jen. Seeing her always lifted my spirits and I could use someone to bounce my theories off and help me figure out what to do next. Mom and Millie were fine to investigate with, but I needed another opinion.

As I started down Main Street toward the post office, my phone pinged. It was Emma. *Just checking in. How you doing?*

How nice was that? My daughter was taking the time out of her busy day to check up on me. Then I frowned. Maybe she'd been talking to Mom again and had gotten an earful of information about dead bodies and potential suspects.

> *I'm great. Don't listen to anything Grandma tells you.*

It took a few seconds for her reply.

> *Lol. I just want you to be safe. Remember, don't jump to conclusions without the proper evidence. That's what I learned in school.*

How the tables had turned. When Emma was a teenager, I'd texted her advice trying to keep her out of trouble, now she was texting it to me. But she had a point. Did I have the proper evidence to suspect the Weatherbys or was I jumping to conclusions?

I won't, don't worry. I'm too busy running the
guesthouse for that.

Okay, so it was a little white lie. Probably no worse than some of the things she'd texted me when she was young. Of course, her reply speared me with guilt.

Okay, Mom. Gotta run. Love you!

Love you too.

I put my phone in my pocket and continued on to the post office, my thoughts swirling about the Weatherbys. I was starting to second-guess myself. What did I really have on the couple? The fact that they didn't know technical information about cameras and had straw and feathers in their room was flimsy at best.

I held open the door of the post office for two senior citizens who were leaving as I was about to enter. Their smiles faded as they recognized me, and they sidled away as if I was contagious.

"Morning Mrs. Fisher and Mrs. Newhart," I said pleasantly.

Mrs. Newhart narrowed her eyes and nodded. Mrs. Fisher grabbed Mrs. Newhart's arm and hauled her down the street. They shuffled off, heads bent together, hose wrinkled around their ankles. I thought I heard some words drift over to me "...heard she was involved in a murder..."

Oh, no. The Oyster Cove rumor mill was in full force

and I was the subject. I shouldn't have been surprised; I knew from past experience that all the good gossip was gleaned down at the post office. All the more reason to help Sheriff Chamberlain along with his investigation. I strode indoors with dogged determination.

Inside, Jen was standing at the counter, a two-foot-high pile of envelopes on her left, a large round stamper on her right and an angry look on her face.

Stamp. Stamp. Stamp.

She plucked envelopes from the top of the stack and hammered the stamper down on them, then piled them on her right.

"What are you doing?" I asked.

She blew a bang out of her eyes. "Stupid postmarking machine broke. I have to do these by hand."

"Can I help?"

She paused the stamping and smiled at me. "No. Thanks for the offer, but I only have one stamper. I could use the company, though, this is boring."

Stamp. Stamp.

"I have some news that will liven things up."

She looked up at me, barely stopping the stamping rhythm. "Oh? Did you figure out who the killer is?"

"Sort of. Remember how I told you about the footprint and the bad review that Charles wrote on the Marinara Mariner?"

"Yep." *Stamp. Stamp.*

"Well, I was partially right."

The stamping stopped and she looked up at me. "Tony really was the killer?"

"No. But it was his footprint."

The stamping resumed. "But he wasn't the killer? What was he doing there?"

I told her about Tony's visit and his and Tina's confession. "I have new suspects now, though. I think it might be the old couple staying at the guesthouse," I said.

"The birdwatchers? Why?"

"According to Flora they had feathers and straw all over their room. You know, like from birds' nests," I said.

Stamp.

"Flora doesn't see too well and she's been known to exaggerate." Jen punctuated her words with more stamping.

"Well, they were seen up at the gulls' nests."

"Why is that unusual? They are birdwatchers, right?"

Stamp. Stamp.

Hmm . . . she had a point. Maybe I was seeing malice where there was none. But they were my only suspects. "Mike said they didn't know the details about one of the cameras they used. That seems odd to me if they are such avid birdwatchers."

Jen stopped stamping and looked up at me with a sly smile. "So you *are* hanging around with Mike."

"No!" Judging by the knowing look Jen gave me, the protest might have been too forceful. I tempered my voice and said matter-of-factly, "He only saw the camera because he's working there and hopefully not for long."

"Uh-huh. Come on, I know you were crushing on him in high school. Admit it. You like having him around."

"That was more than twenty years ago. I've been

married since. Who lingers on their high-school crush anyway?"

She looked at me skeptically then went back to stamping. "Just because you were married to a jerk shouldn't sour you on men. Look at all the jerks I dated before I found the right guy."

Jen wasn't joking, she had dated a lot of jerks, but now she was with her soulmate. I was a little envious of their wedded bliss, but also doubtful that would happen for me. I was no spring chicken. "I don't think I'm ready for dating."

"Ohhh, so there's a chance you might be someday. Good, I'll keep that in mind."

"Great. So back to the case…"

"Right." She made a face as if trying to remember the specifics. "What about the sabotage? Could Ron have done that?"

I'd wondered that myself, but it wasn't like it took a lot of strength or skill to do that sawing. One would have to know where to make the cuts, but it wasn't rocket science. "Maybe Ron was a carpenter. I mean, he certainly could have sabotaged the room *and* he made a remark about small-town police not following up thoroughly, so I wonder if he was banking on the fact that Seth Chamberlain might not even notice the sabotage and rule it an accident."

Jen stopped stamping and thought about it. "I guess that is a lot of counts against them. I just can't believe those nice people could be killers. The Wessons were so nice."

"Wessons? You mean Weatherbys."

She scrunched up her face. "No. Wesson. They came in to pick up a package the other day and I'm certain that was the name on it."

"No. They signed in as Weatherby. It was on his license."

Jen's brows shot up. "What if they have a fake identity? If they are the killers, they might be pretending to be someone else."

"Why? I doubt they came here knowing they would kill someone." Then again, if they came knowing they were going to poison the gulls, maybe they did use a fake identity.

"Serial seagull killers? Who knows? With fake names they can kill off whole colonies of gulls and then disappear and no one can trace it back to them."

That made sense to me. "You could be on to something. There is definitely something suspicious about the old couple."

"There's only one way to find out what it is."

"What's that?"

"Follow them around and see what they do. If they killed Charles because he discovered they were doing something shady, and they didn't leave town right away, then chances are they are still doing it."

Chapter Seventeen

Nero shrunk back into the doorway of the bookstore as Josie came out of the post office. "Get back! She'll see us!"

Marlowe crouched low beside him. Juliette, Boots, Stubbs, Poe, and Harry just looked at him.

"So what if she sees you?" Stubbs asked.

"We don't want her to think we're following her."

"Ahh...Still playing aloof?" Juliette preened.

"Yep. Plus we don't want her to try to lock us up inside or anything. We need to be free to protect her," Marlowe said.

All the cats shuddered at the thought of being shut up inside. Sure, many humans tried to curtail their outdoor activities, thinking it was in their best interest, and it likely was for *regular* cats. But Nero and his gang were special and needed to be free to roam around. How else would they solve mysteries?

"Especially since I feel she may be barking up the wrong tree." Nero peeked out from his hiding spot. Josie was almost a block away. He slipped out and trotted a few stores down, taking care to stick close to the edge of the buildings and duck into doorways when possible. The others followed.

"Barking up the wrong tree?" Poe asked. "Sounds like something that Mrs. Peterson's chihuahua would do."

"I've seen him do that a few times," Harry said.

"Very funny." Boots ran his paw the length of his long whiskers, curling them up at the end with a flourish. "Nero means that he thinks Josie is on the wrong track. Why don't you fill us in, Nero?"

"There was an incident at the guesthouse last night that eliminated some of the suspects." Nero told them how Tony had come to the guesthouse and what happened after. Admittedly, he might have embellished the whole confrontation part a little bit to make it seem like he and Marlowe had stopped Tony from harming Josie, but since Marlowe didn't disagree he felt like he was within his rights. He certainly *would* have if it had come to that.

"Darn. I thought that clog print was a surefire clue and Tony would take the rap. So now what?" Stubbs asked.

"Once Tony was cleared, we knew Josie had to go back to the earlier clue. The note." Nero ducked quickly behind a tree when Josie turned around. "Holy hiss, did she see us?"

Marlowe, who had ducked right behind him, peered out. "I don't think so. Looks like she's getting into her car."

"Hmm...I wish I knew where she was going." Nero narrowed his gaze at Josie, who was settling in behind the wheel of her twelve-year-old Dodge sedan.

"Hopefully back to the guesthouse," Harry said.

"We can take the shortcut back there," Nero suggested.

"Did you convince her to look at the note? I thought the police had it," Boots said.

Marlowe nodded. "It took quite a bit of effort, but she finally got the hint. Luckily she had a picture of it on her phone."

"So what happened? Don't tell me the note was a bum steer," Stubbs said, using his hard-boiled detective lingo again.

"She puzzled out the potential meanings of the letters," Nero said.

"Josie seems quite adept at word puzzles and games. I've seen her do the crosswords before," Marlowe added.

"She discovered something?" Juliette asked.

"Now she suspects the Weatherbys. I feel she might be getting into dangerous territory, though, and want to keep her close." Josie's car pulled onto the road and Nero dove under a shrub, scaring the bejesus out of a sparrow who burst out the other side like he'd been shot from a cannon.

"Are you sure she's correct in suspecting the Weatherbys?" Boots asked. "My whiskers are tingling at the thought and not in a good way."

"There are some clues. We saw gull feathers and nesting material in their room," Marlowe said.

"And I saw them near the gulls' nests," Juliette added.

"They do seem overly interested in the gulls and Josie thought the note might be a blackmail note because Charles caught someone messing around with the gulls somehow," Nero said.

"You mean this all has to do with what is happening to the gulls?" Harry asked.

"It's a possibility." Nero scrambled out from under the

bush and shook errant leaves off his coat, then started to groom off any dirt that might have gotten on the white patch of his chest. "Whatever the real reason is, Josie is determined to find the killer. Her reputation is on the line, after all."

"Of course. And we must assist like we always do."

"Great. Well, we gotta run." Nero trotted off in the direction of the shortcut that led to the guesthouse. "I'll keep you all posted."

"Let us know if we can do anything else!" Poe yelled after him.

"You know where to find us!" Harry added.

"I'll be watching the cliff from the belfry!" Juliette purred.

Nero broke into a full run, Marlowe at his tail. If they hurried they could get back to the guesthouse before Josie did something that might put herself in danger.

*

I waited almost all day for the Weatherbys to make a move. I hovered around the front rooms with my duster, trying to look busy. I wanted to stay near the foyer so I could catch them if they left, but there was only so much dusting and straightening one could do in the front rooms.

I felt a little like a creep. Was I doing the right thing? If they were innocent, I'd simply see them taking pictures of birds. But if not...

I'd also had the distinct feeling someone...or something...was following me when I left the post office earlier that day. I hadn't seen anyone when I did a tricky glance over my shoulders and the Weatherbys' car was parked and cold (yes, I felt the hood) when I got back to the guesthouse, so it wasn't them. What if *they* weren't the killers and it was the real killer who was following me?

The cats had been acting strangely too. They bolted into the house a few minutes after I got home and had been staring at me the whole time. Now all of a sudden they'd disappeared. A creak on the stairs brought me out of my reverie.

"Oh, hi, Josie. Huh, I saw Flora cleaning in here earlier." Ron looked at me suspiciously. "How often do you have to dust this place?"

"One can never have things too clean!" I chirped. "Old houses collect lots of dust."

"Ahem. Right. Well the Mrs. and I are just going for a walk." Ron held up the camera that dangled around his neck. "Going to see if we can spot a blue-billed horn-swallow."

"They have those around here?" I'd never actually heard of one. Was he making it up? If he was the killer, then he probably was. I remembered how Mike had said that he thought it was odd that Ron had the specifications of his camera wrong, maybe he'd been lying then too? Maybe if I'd listened to Mike, I would have realized Ron could be the killer sooner. Of course, I would never tell Mike that.

"They are very rare, but we're hopeful!" Iona pulled Ron toward the door and I stared out the window as they headed off to the path at the edge of the estate property. It wound up the hill above the Smugglers Bay

Inn, then over to the cliffs near the gulls. I tossed down my feather duster and followed.

I'd always liked the serenity of walking in the woods with only the chipmunks and birds as company. The smell of pine and the dapples of sunlight filtering through the leaves can be magical. Except not today. Today the woods had an ominous feeling and being alone wasn't quite so serene.

I came to a fork in the path. Now, which trail had they taken? I squinted down the path on the right and caught sight of something red moving in between the trees. Iona's shirt. I picked up the pace. Something dark ran in front of me, almost tripping me.

"Whoa!"

Mew! Nero leapt onto a rock and preened.

"Hey, watch it." I whispered because I didn't want to alert the Weatherbys to my presence.

Purrr. Marlowe did figure-eights around my ankles.

"Get lost. Shoo. I'm busy." I stepped over her and continued on the path, slowing when I came to the corner. I didn't want the Weatherbys to see me if they'd slowed down. And surely they must have slowed, because we were going uphill. I know *I* felt like slowing down, and they were a lot older. I could probably take my time and let them get to the cliffs and still see them doing something nefarious. But what if they also did something along the way? I didn't want to miss that.

Meow! Nero shot ahead of me on the path then stopped, almost blocking it.

"Look out," I whispered, stepping over him again. Darn cats were going to ruin everything.

I turned the corner. No Weatherbys. I went a little faster now, afraid I might miss out on something.

Nero and Marlowe trotted in front of me in the most annoying way possible. It was almost as if they were trying to trip me.

Another splash of red! They were just ahead. I didn't want to lose them, but also couldn't let them know that I was here.

I continued on, craning to see ahead. They were probably around the next corner. I rounded cautiously.

No one was there.

I picked up the pace. Maybe the next corner.

Nope. Where were they? Had I lost them? And where were the cats? They'd run off and—

"Josie. What brings you out here?"

I spun around to see Ron and Iona Weatherby blocking the path.

"Josie. What a surprise!" Iona really did look surprised, but how had they gotten behind me without seeing me on the path? And why would they double back and then come up behind me? Had they seen me following them and come to confront me? Would I be their next victim? I tensed, ready to flee. Too bad they were blocking the way. I had nowhere to go but toward the cliff. Images of my body smashed on the rocks came to mind.

Mew.

Nero, the traitor, was threading between Iona's ankles and she bent down to pet him.

"We didn't realize you were a nature lover." Ron stepped closer, a look of suspicion on his face.

"I am. Really. But I don't get much time to enjoy it what with all my duties at the guesthouse," I stuttered as I tried to plan my escape. I could dart around the big pine, jump over that fallen oak and crash through the woods to connect with the trail below. They were old, I could outrun them.

Meow! Nero trotted over to Ron and gave him the same purring ankle-rubbing routine.

"Yes, of course," Ron said. "But you do come out here often?"

"Uh huh... Yep."

"I suppose you go up to the cliff?" Iona straightened from where she'd crouched to pet the cat and brushed her hands together. "The view is outstanding."

"Yes, of course. Who wouldn't? Is that where you go?" While I was stuck here, I might as well ask them some questions and see if I could trip them up.

"Oh yes." Ron hefted the camera. "Birdwatching."

"The gulls?" I tried to keep my voice casual.

Ron's brow furrowed. "What do you know about the gulls?"

Aha! I could tell by the way he asked that he was worried. His tone definitely indicated guilt. But I had to be careful. If they had killed Charles as I suspected, they probably wouldn't hesitate to kill me.

I shrugged as if I had no suspicions at all. "They nest up there. It's sad what's happening to them, but that's nature, I guess."

"What do you mean?" Iona asked innocently.

Trying to play dumb? Well, two could play at that game. "They're dying at an alarming rate. I guess it's just a cycle of nature. Not enough food to support the growth of the colony."

Ron and Iona exchanged a glance. Had I fooled them? Now was my chance to get away. Nero and Marlowe had trotted back on the path and were looking over their shoulders at me. Yep, that was my cue to leave.

"Oh, look at the time!" I glanced at my wrist. "The cats are signaling that they need their afternoon meal." I pointed toward the two cats who were staring at us.

Ron and Iona looked dubious but they stood aside. "Of course, dear. You shouldn't delay their feeding. Too bad you won't make it to the cliff. Seems a waste to come halfway up and not get to the top."

Yeah, too bad because that would be a great place to push me off. "I know, but I live here so I get to go anytime I want. You two enjoy!" I hurried off without looking back.

Only when I was a safe distance away did I turn around. Judging by the way those two had been acting, my suspicions were confirmed that they were the culprits. But what should I do about that? I couldn't tell Seth Chamberlain until I had some concrete proof. He'd never listen, especially after I'd messed up by pointing the finger at Tony. I was going to have to resort to breaking into their rooms and looking around.

Chapter Eighteen

Later that afternoon, I made sure the Weatherbys saw the big coupon for the senior special at Salty's Crab Shack that night. Since I didn't serve dinner it was a sure bet they'd be dining out. I waited a few minutes after they drove off just to make sure they didn't turn back.

Once all the guests were out to dinner, I rushed up the stairs, tamping down the guilt that was spreading in my chest as I fingered the spare key to the Weatherbys' room. I'd only ever used the room key for cleaning, and this felt like a violation. I reminded myself that the nice old couple could be hardened killers and looking in their room was necessary to find evidence.

I was bent over the keyhole and had assured myself this was the right thing to do when I heard, "What are you doing?"

Dang! I'd been so focused on sneaking around that I hadn't noticed Mike coming down the hall. He had his tool belt and a dark gray T-shirt that showed off the fact that he still kept in shape even after being out of the navy for several years. Not that I was noticing.

I straightened and leaned against the wall casually as if breaking into guests' rooms was nothing out of the ordinary. "Cleaning."

He glanced at the door. "Isn't that the Weatherbys' room?"

"Yep. Still needs to be cleaned."

He leaned his shoulder against the wall so he was facing me and cocked his head. "I thought Flora did the cleaning."

I snorted. "Seriously?"

"Yeah, I guess maybe she doesn't do all of it." His eyes narrowed. "But you wouldn't be doing some snooping in there, would you?"

I tried to look incredulous. "Me? I would never snoop on guests. Why would I?"

"Aunt Millie told me all about the new theory you guys have come up with that Charles was blackmailing someone. She said you suspected the Weatherbys."

Dang. Millie had a big mouth.

"Maybe." I studied him for a second. He had been an investigator in the navy and had been acting like he was interested in this case. Maybe he had an opinion. And since I wasn't one-hundred-percent sure about the Weatherbys, maybe I should listen to it. "What do you think?"

He shrugged. "Might be a good deduction, but I don't think they did it. The sabotage of the stairs doesn't seem like their forte."

I leaned closer to him and lowered my voice. "But you said they acted suspiciously about the cameras."

He inched closer and my heartbeat sped up. "Yeah, I did. But whether it is or isn't them, *you* shouldn't be investigating it. Leave it to Sheriff Chamberlain."

I sighed. "I wish I could, but he seems to be barking up the wrong tree and I'm sitting on the top branch."

Mike's face softened. "I know. Don't worry. The truth will come out. I've been looking into it myself, so you don't need to concern yourself with it."

I didn't need to concern myself? Did he seriously just say that? Did he think I should keep to the cooking and cleaning and let the men do the investigating? Ha! I'd show him. But I didn't voice my thoughts. Better to let him think I was playing along with him. I knew how to handle domineering, control-freaky men.

I smiled sweetly. "That's really nice of you. I suppose you're right. Thanks. Now if you don't mind…" I gestured toward the door.

"Right, you have cleaning. You work really hard here. Maybe you need a night out."

Not with you. No way. "Maybe."

"I'm just finishing up here and…"

He let his voice drift off and an eager puppy-dog look spread across his face. I knew what he was suggesting but I would not be swayed. He probably just wanted to get me away from the Weatherbys' room so I wouldn't get evidence that they were the killers before he did. I knew how competitive men could be. Besides, I had no desire to go on a date. Not with him or anyone for that matter. For one, I was still reeling after the divorce, and for two, we had history and it wasn't all pretty.

"You must be almost done with the work Millie contracted you to do," I said by way of avoiding his suggestion.

Mike nodded, looking kind of sad. "This place needs a lot more work, though. I have spare time in my schedule…"

"Thanks, but I have a tight budget." The last thing I wanted was Mike hanging around here. As it was, I was almost starting to get used to him and I certainly did not want that. I didn't want to hurt his feelings, but I'd already been talking to Ed O'Hara—a nice retired gentleman who was not within my dating range—about doing the rest of the work.

He leaned in. "I'd be willing to give you a discount or we could work something out."

He was magnetic, with a charming smile and soulful brown eyes. A discount would be nice. So would...wait! No. I was not going to go there. Best if he was out of my sight for good.

"I wouldn't want to take advantage of you, but thanks for the offer." I gestured toward the door. "I really need to get to work."

He pushed away from the wall, obviously disappointed. "OK. But I hope you really are cleaning. I'm serious, Josie, there's a killer on the loose and it could be dangerous."

"Just cleaning." I smiled and managed to hold his gaze until he walked away. Once I heard the last stair creak, I let out my breath. I didn't like being sneaky or lying, but one did what one had to do.

I slipped the key into the lock, turned the knob, and the door squeaked open.

Given Flora's description, I had expected the room to be filled with feathers and straw, but it was neat as a pin. Maybe Flora *had* cleaned. Most likely she'd exaggerated. I poked around in the bureau, under the bed, and in the medicine cabinet.

The sound of tires on gravel startled me and I ran to the window. It was only Mike leaving. The driveway was empty. The Weatherbys' car was still gone, but I knew I had to hurry.

In the small drawer of the writing desk, I hit pay dirt. An envelope addressed to Bill and Cindy Wesson. Hmm...maybe I was on to something, but I needed more. Maybe in the closet or between the mattress and box spring?

I was on my hands and knees in the closet, examining the bottom of Ron's shoes, which had straw and twigs embedded inside the thick treads, when I heard the door open.

"I've been craving clams ever since—" Iona's words were cut off as she noticed me crouched there on the floor. "Josie? What are you doing?"

"Ummm...just cleaning."

Her questioning gaze was riveted on my right hand, which still held Ron's shoe.

"I like to vacuum under the shoes." I plopped the shoe back down and jumped up. "See? All nice and clean."

Ron closed the door and glared at me. His eyes were not friendly. "I don't see any vacuum cleaner."

Crap. Maybe Mike had been right and I should have stayed out of investigating. But if I didn't, I'd have to remember to bring props next time if I was trying to pose with a cleaning excuse.

"I prefer the old-fashioned method of picking stuff up by hand."

Mew!

The cats must have snuck in with the Weatherbys. They trotted around Iona's feet, looking up at the bag of takeout food from Salty's that was filling the room with the delicious smell of fried clams. Just my luck they'd decided to get takeout instead of eat in.

Meow!

Nero cast a glance at me. Was he trying to signal me? To let me know they would help me escape if need be? Because judging by the way Ron was planted in front of the door with his hands on his hips, I might need help.

Iona put the bag on the dresser and Marlowe immediately jumped up and started sniffing.

Iona glared at me. No longer did she look like a sweet old lady. "Looks like you didn't rush home to feed the cats like you said you were going to do when we saw you out in the woods. This one appears to be starving."

"Oh, them." I waved my hand dismissively at the cats. "They beg for food all the time."

I inched toward the doorway. Maybe I could rush Ron and knock him over? I hated to knock over a senior citizen, but he was a killer.

"No sense in lying, Josie. We know what you were up to out in the woods," Ron said.

So they knew I was on to them. Fine! I'd get myself out of this somehow.

Mew!

Nero jumped up on the dresser and sniffed.

Iona snatched up the bag. "I don't think fried clams are good for cats."

Lovely, a senior citizen killer who cared about cat nutrition.

"That's right. I'll just take them downstairs for some properly formulated cat food." I glanced at Nero and Marlowe. Not sure what I was expecting. Maybe for them to distract the Weatherbys while I made a break for it? But they were more interested in the takeout bag because now they were sitting at Iona's feet practically begging like dogs.

"Nice try, Josie. You might as well confess. We aren't letting you go." Ron stood firmly in front of the door.

Images of my body at the bottom of the stairs in the west wing bubbled up. I hadn't heard any other cars pull in, so it was likely no one else was home. Why hadn't I listened to Mike? I decided to buy some time.

I crossed my arms over my chest. "You confess first. I know what you've been up to."

Ron and Iona glanced at each other. "You do? How did you find out?"

"Process of elimination," I said proudly. But not too proudly, lest it anger them and make their killing method more painful.

Meroo…

Nero tore his attention from the bag long enough to blink at me. Was that some kind of signal? Too bad I didn't understand cat-blink.

I moved toward the door another inch. Maybe it was best to let them take me to the west wing. That way I'd have more opportunities to escape. Or maybe I should try to reason with them? Convince them to give themselves up.

"What are you going to do? Push me down the stairs and try to make it look like an accident? I don't think the police will fall for that again."

"What are you talking about?" Iona looked confused.

"Don't play dumb. I know the truth and what you've been up to. But you can't kill me like you did Charles. It won't work. Might be easier to give yourselves up. I'm sure it was an accident. The cops will go easy, but if you kill me too . . . not so much."

"What are you talking about? Why would we have killed Charles?" Ron asked.

"To cover up the fact that you were messing with the gulls, of course."

Ron and Iona looked nervous. Clearly I'd hit a nerve. They hadn't figured that I'd discovered their secret about the gulls.

Meroo!

Marlowe and Nero sat at Iona's feet, tails swishing back and forth anxiously. Eyes focused on the bag of clams. Fine friends they were. Here I was about to be murdered and all they could think about was clams.

"Oh, for crying out loud, give them a clam," Ron said to Iona as he took a step toward me. I backed up. "Now, Josie, I see what you are trying to do but it won't work."

Darn! He was on to my ploy to keep them talking and try to edge toward the door. Now what? I glanced back at the window, but we were on the second floor. Maybe I could lock myself in the bathroom?

"You're not going to get away with murder. Think about it."

"Why do you keep saying that?" Iona had taken a clam out of the bag, picked off the coating and was feeding little pieces to the cats. They were lapping it up, not paying any attention to the dire circumstances going on around them. "It's no use trying to cover up what you've been doing."

I frowned. "What *I've* been doing?"

"Yes, dear." Ron managed to look fatherly. "It's quite obvious that you're the one who has been killing the gulls. Earlier when we caught you in the woods, we know you were going to the nests, but turned back because you ran into us. I don't know what happened with that Charles fellow but if you just confess, I think we can convince the authorities to go easy on you."

"What I don't understand is why you would do it. Were the gulls hurting business at the guesthouse?" Iona tossed a tiny clam morsel to Nero, who caught it midair like a dog.

This was confusing. What was their angle? Would they try to blame me for their crime? Maybe they were trying to force a confession like I was doing to them. I fisted my hands on my hips and stood my ground. "I had nothing to do with the gulls. They aren't hurting business at all. They don't even come here." I gestured toward the window where a few evening gulls were circling far over the water, as if to prove my point.

Iona popped a clam in her mouth and exchanged a confused look with Ron. "Well then, why harm them?"

"It's not me, it's you!"

Ron shook his head and gave me a sad look of pity, then reached in the bag for a clam. "Think about it, this has been happening long before we came. It's not us."

I still didn't believe him. "How do I know you

weren't in town staying somewhere else before? And what about the fact that you have been lurking up near the gulls. You don't know the specifics of your camera and had straw and twigs from the gulls' nests in your shoes!"

Ha! Now I had him.

Ron glanced at Iona. "Looks like we better enact plan B."

He advanced toward me, a serious look on his face. Ooops, now I'd done it. I stepped back, but the dresser stopped me from going further. He kept coming. My heart thudded against my chest as I searched for a means of escape.

I glanced at Iona for help. I mean, I know she was in cahoots with him but maybe she'd have pity on a fellow woman.

Too late. He was almost on me. He reached out as if to grab me, I dodged left, threw myself on the floor and tucked into a roll.

To my surprise he didn't lunge for me. Instead he gave me a funny look and opened the bureau drawer.

He fished underneath. Probably where he kept a gun!

I squeezed my eyes shut and threw my arm across my face as if that might stop a bullet. "Don't shoot!"

"Shoot? Josie, dear, what are you talking about?" Iona asked.

I opened my eyes. Ron was standing in front of me, a yellow padded mailer in his hand. He reached in and pulled out what looked like a wallet. He flipped it open. Inside was a gold badge and ID card.

"You didn't believe us, so I wanted to prove to you why we were here and why we can't possibly be the ones who have been harming the gulls." Ron handed over the badge.

It looked official, but I'd never heard of the department. "U. S. Department of Audubon Investigations?"

Ron and Iona nodded. "Yes. We're investigators for a special government division. Not a lot of people know there is a department of Audubon Investigations. We often get confused with the Audubon Society, but we have no relation to that. You were right about one thing, we aren't here as regular guests. We were sent to investigate what's happening with the gulls."

"And our names aren't Ron and Iona Weatherby either." Iona picked a clam out of the bag and passed it to Ron. "It's Bill and Cindy Wesson and I'm sorry to tell you, but you're looking mighty suspicious right now."

"Especially since we caught you skulking around in the woods today and looking very guilty," Ron added.

Iona nodded. "And the way you ran off after we caught you...well, you can see why we think you're the culprit."

I sank down on the bed. Ron and Iona (yes, I still thought of them as their fake names) were government agents? Even worse, they suspected me! I supposed I had been acting funny in the woods, but that was only because I thought they were killers. "I was guilty. But not of doing anything to the gulls. I was following you because I thought *you* were doing something to them!"

The cats purred around my ankles as I told Ron and

Iona about the note and my suspicions that Charles wasn't killed because of a review, but because he was blackmailing someone.

"And you thought he was blackmailing us?" Iona chewed thoughtfully. "Well, I suppose I can see why. We were going off and watching the gulls every day, but that was for research, of course you didn't know that."

"And we did investigate the nests," Ron said. "Funny thing, we didn't find anything wrong. We suspect someone is somehow poisoning the gulls. We've been trying to figure out where you kept the poison so we could confiscate it for evidence and turn it over to the police."

"Well, it's not me," I said. "I mean, why would I? The gulls are not a nuisance to me and why would I kill Charles and put the reputation of the guesthouse in jeopardy?"

"Good point." Iona sat on the bed beside me, passed me the clams and patted my knee. "Besides you're not the killing type. Gull or human. And we've seen a lot of killers, haven't we, dear?" She looked up at Ron, who nodded.

"I was afraid we were on the wrong track with you, anyway," Ron said. "We had no evidence that you even went near the cliff until we saw you on the path. And, as you said, you have no motive."

Iona nodded. "But when we ran into you on the path, we started to second-guess ourselves. Funny that it turns out you were looking for the same person we were."

I fished around in the bag and picked out a clam with a big belly. I paused before scarfing it down. "Well, if it's not you and it's not me, then who is it?"

Chapter Nineteen

Nero's mouth watered as he watched Josie eat the succulent clam with the plump belly. "I wish they'd pass some of those to us."

"Yeah, what gives? The lady was feeding us until they sorted things out." Marlowe watched Josie pass the bag to Ron. "It's like they've forgotten all about us. Maybe I should hawk up a hairball."

"No, they don't like it when that happens around food." Nero sighed, and hopped down from the bed. "I'm just glad they've straightened things out."

"Yeah, I was sure there would be a problem when Josie followed them through the woods."

"Me too, especially since she wasn't understanding our hints about turning back."

Marlowe preened her belly. "It did seem as if she was turning to us for help a little while ago here in the room, though."

"Yet she didn't 'get' the hint that we were not concerned and she shouldn't be either." The clam bag crinkled and Nero looked up at the humans. They were seated side by side on the bed, no longer paying attention to the cats. Had they eaten all the clams?

"I think we need to figure out who has a vested interest in getting rid of the gulls," Ron said.

"Are we really sure the gulls' plight is connected to Charles's death?" Iona glanced at Nero. He willed her to pick out another clam for him and she did! But just so the humans didn't think they were too eager, he let it drop on the floor before sniffing at it disdainfully for a few seconds, then hunkering down and eating it slowly.

"I get the next one," Marlowe said.

"Fine, but we can't waste too much time eating. We have to point them toward the real suspect." Nero swallowed the last tidbit and licked his lips.

"Maybe it doesn't have anything to do with the gulls. I could have been wrong about the letter. I mean it was only a few parts of words," Josie said.

"What were the parts?" Ron asked.

While Josie fished out her phone and showed the Weatherbys the picture of the note, Nero got to work trying to give them a hint. Who was the killer and what were they doing with the gulls? Now that it had been proven not to be the Weatherbys, Nero could think of only one person it could be.

He hopped up on the old cast-iron steam radiator under the window. Luckily it was summer and the heat wasn't on, otherwise he would surely have burned his paws. As it was, the radiator, with its fancy accordion of scrolled pipes, was not very comfortable. It was just another one of the sacrifices cats had to make for their humans. "The humans are asking the same question we asked ourselves earlier. Maybe this time Josie will listen and come to the same conclusion."

Meroo!

"Oh, shush now, you've had more than your share

of clams." Iona waved a dismissive hand at him without even looking in his direction.

"I think I'm going to need help," Nero said to Marlowe.

Marlowe joined him on the radiator. She sat and curled her tail around him, then looked out toward the cove, her whiskers twitching. The moon was out and the last gull had gone wherever gulls go at night. But hopefully Josie would get their drift.

Merooo!

Mewo!

Merowl!

"What's going on? Is something out there?" Josie came to join them at the window, petting the top of Nero's head. He had to admit it felt good. He let down his guard and purred a few times.

Mew! Marlowe signaled that she wanted attention too, but she kept her eyes on the cove.

"Something sure must be interesting out there." Josie petted Marlowe, giving her equal attention. "What do you see?" Josie stared out the window. "Oh, I think I've got it!"

"What's that?" Ron asked.

Josie whirled around. "Stella Dumont runs the Smugglers Bay Inn over there. The gulls have been hanging around her deck and pooping all over it."

"Really?" Iona and Ron joined Josie, squinting out into the night.

"Not only that, but Stella has been seen lurking around here," Josie said.

"And Charles was killed here," Ron added.

"Do you think Charles caught Stella doing something to harm the gulls?" Iona asked.

"I wouldn't put it past her to do that. Or to kill Charles," Josie said.

Nero and Marlowe hopped down from the radiator, their tails held high proudly. Finally, Josie had gotten their hint and now it was up to the humans to catch the killer.

*

"I *knew* it was Stella," I said. "I should have trusted my first instincts, but I thought it had something to do with Charles's cookbook. When I found out that it was Tina who took it, I ruled Stella out."

"But what proof do we have?" Iona peered out the window as if the answer was out there somewhere.

"Well, she does have a problem with the gulls," Ron said. "Remember when we went there for lunch and a gull pooped in your clam chowder?"

Iona made a face. "Yeah. Nasty."

"And my maid saw her skulking around here." Josie pressed her lips together. "I don't remember if she said it was the night Charles died. I'll have to ask."

"That does seem like a start. But it's not enough to call the sheriff on." Ron's words dashed my hopes.

"But we have to do *something*," I said.

"Indeed." Ron tapped his lips with his finger. "What we need is to set a trap and let her walk right into it and prove her guilt."

"Like what?" Iona asked.

"Something that would be irresistible to the killer.

Something that would make them expose themselves somehow."

I snapped my fingers. "Got it! What if we say we found a clue in the room where Charles was killed and when the police run forensics on it, it will leave no doubt who murdered Charles."

"Like what? DNA? A fingerprint?" Ron asked.

"Maybe."

"We might not have to be too specific," Iona said. "We can avoid the details, just a hint is better."

"But how do we get this information to the killer?"

"This is a small town and, unless I am out of touch, if there is something juicy to talk about, there are certain circles where you can let the secret out and it will be around town in no time." Iona glanced at me and I nodded.

"Good," Ron said. "Here's what we need to do. We'll start a rumor that you've found a clue to the killer's identity. It's in the west wing where Charles was killed."

"And the killer will come to find it before the police!" Iona said.

I frowned. "That won't work, the killer isn't just going to waltz into a guesthouse full of people."

Ron's eyes gleamed. "Not with a guesthouse full of people. But everyone knows that you don't serve dinner. Can you arrange something in town where your guests get a discount somewhere tomorrow night? We'll help make sure everyone goes out to take advantage of it." Ron pointed to the clam bag. "You know, like you made it so obvious that there was a special at Salty's."

My cheeks prickled with heat. Had I been that

obvious? Is that why Ron and Iona had gotten takeout? Oh, well, it all worked out in the end. "I think I can arrange something. Tony down at the Marinara Mariner owes me one."

I could maybe get him to make a special twenty-percent-off coupon for the guests in exchange for making sure no one ever found out about him and Tina. Blackmail? Sure. But it was for a good cause.

"And one more thing to make it irresistible," Ron said. "When you are spreading the rumor, make sure it is known that you will be out of town until the next morning, but the guesthouse will remain unlocked so that your guests can come and go after dinner."

"Okay," I said.

"Good, maybe if you can get that rumor started tomorrow morning, we can have our killer in handcuffs by tomorrow night."

"Sounds good," I said. "I know exactly where to start."

Chapter Twenty

The next morning I was up with the gulls. Looking at them through the kitchen window, I wondered if they would stop dying off once Stella was in jail. There were only two over her deck now and I swear a month ago there would be six or seven in the morning.

Now what for breakfast? I wished I hadn't spent so much time trying to come up with the best way to spread the rumor and sweet-talking Tony into getting me coupons last night. Mom and Millie had picked them up and were supposed to deliver them here any minute.

I was rummaging through the recipe file—still no sour-cream coffee cake—when I heard a tap on the kitchen door.

Mom and Millie were outside with sneaky looks on their faces, glancing back behind them and whispering. I motioned for them to come in and the door squeaked as Millie opened it. I made a mental note to oil the hinges later on, or whatever one did for squeaky doors. I had enough going on right now.

Millie presented the coupons from the Marinara Mariner. "Tony made these up special, just like you asked him to."

"He was very nice to us." Mom leaned in and whispered, "Didn't want us to tell his little secret."

The cats trotted over and purred at Millie's feet while she fed them some sort of fishy-smelling treats. I didn't have those types of treats here for them and I wondered if she'd been holding out on me and keeping the most savory treats for herself so she would still be their favorite.

Millie scowled at the stove, peeked in the oven and then turned her frown on me. "You haven't started breakfast yet?"

"I was just trying to figure out what to cook."

Millie glanced at her watch. "It's almost seven thirty, not much time to make something." She pressed her lips together and glanced at the pantry. "Hmm...I know. Do you have any breakfast ham?"

I glanced in the fridge. Two ham patties sat wrapped in their plastic covering. "Yep."

"Good, then we'll make ham-and-cheese muffin puffs. It will only take twenty minutes and the guests love them." Millie rushed into the pantry and grabbed the Bisquick. "Get out the ham and some eggs, milk, cheese and olive oil."

I did as I was told and twenty minutes later the kitchen was filled with the smell of homemade biscuits. Millie pulled the golden biscuits with pink dots of ham and gooey cheese out of the oven. I added a fruit bowl, milk and cereal and we headed to the dining room where the guests had already gathered.

Ron and Iona shot me a knowing look. Tina gave me a nervous glance. About the only one I didn't have a secret with was Ava. She was looking around with a twinkle in her eye as if she was on to the fact that there were questionable goings on at the guesthouse.

"I have a nice surprise for everyone," I announced, after I'd laid the food out and they were milling about the buffet table making their selections. I held up the coupons. "The Marinara Mariner has offered a wonderful twenty-percent discount on dinner between seven and nine tonight for guests of the Oyster Cove Guesthouse only."

"The food there is wonderful," Ron said.

"That's a good deal," Iona added.

"Marinara gives me heartburn." Ava squinted at the coupon.

"I've never heard of the place, is it good?" Tina's demeanor dripped with faux innocence but her sideways glance told me that Tony had already alerted her to my blackmail demand.

"Yes. And since Josie has to go out of town tonight, it will be good for you all to have a night out. The guesthouse will be unlocked for you when you get back," Millie said.

Ava's eyes narrowed. "So, would the last person in lock the front door, then?"

That stumped me. "Err... that's not necessary. It's not like someone is going to break in and steal things. Very low crime here." Except for the recent murder. "And, of course, your individual rooms are locked, so no one can go in them."

Ava studied me for a few beats then nodded. "Okay then. Sounds good. I do have a hankering for garlic bread."

With breakfast served and the dirty deed done, I headed back to the kitchen with Mom and Millie. I didn't have time to waste. I had to get to the post office during peak gossip hours in time to let the news that the guesthouse would be empty and unlocked make its way to the killer.

*

The post office was always the most crowded at 11 a.m., so I timed it to get there then. I wanted to maximize the number of people who overheard me to ensure the rumor got spread around quickly. I knew that Stella liked to keep track of everything that went on around town, so I was positive it would get back to her.

"Hey, Josie." Jen looked over at me as she wrestled Priority Mail tape onto a ginormous package that little old gray-haired Lottie Cox had hefted onto the counter.

"Hi, Jen! I just stopped in to say goodbye before my trip tonight."

"You're going on a trip?"

"Just overnight. Be back in the morning."

"Umm…okay." She put the last of the tape on the package and punched something into the postal machine, then turned to Lottie. "That will be twenty-three dollars and twenty-one cents."

"Twenty-three dollars and twenty-one cents!" Lottie clutched her purse against her chest. "Highway robbery!"

"Sorry, Lottie, but I don't set the prices. I could send it regular mail?"

Lottie's lips pursed. "How long would that take?"

Jen consulted the screen in front of her. "Seven days."

"Forget it." Lottie creaked open her purse and counted out the money. "Darn government is getting greedy."

While Jen completed the transaction, I continued, "Yeah, so my guests are eating at the Mariner tonight. Tony has a special coupon just for the Oyster Cove Guesthouse. Isn't that nice?"

Jen's left brow quirked up at the mention of Tony. "All the guests?"

I hadn't yet filled her in on the fact that I'd discovered the Weatherbys' true identity and our plan to dupe Stella into revealing herself as the killer. "Yep. And it's a shame I have to go away too because I may have found an important clue as to the identity of the person who killed Charles Prescott."

The hubbub of conversation among the post-office customers stopped.

"A clue? Like what?" Jen asked.

"I can't really say, but the police are meeting me tomorrow morning to take it. I'd do it tonight but already had the plans to go away."

"Right. Plans. So, I guess the guesthouse will be empty?" Jen said loudly. She'd been a quick study in high school and apparently that hadn't changed. She must have caught on to my intentions.

"Yep, exactly." I winked to thank her.

"Did you have something to mail?" she asked, because I was standing there holding up the line.

"Huh? Oh, no…Ummm…Just came to check my post-office box. You know, because I'm going out of town tonight." I made a big show of going over to the post-office box. I tried to keep the smile off my face as I heard people mumbling about the big clue and the guesthouse, how I was going out of town and how it wasn't fair that Tony Murano had given a special coupon to only my guests.

The box was full of fliers, so I tugged them out and went over to dump them in the bin that the post office kept against the wall for such things. My way was blocked by Mike Sullivan. Arms crossed over his chest, eyes narrowed. He looked suspicious. Probably that navy-investigator training.

"What's this about you going out of town, Sunshine? Aunt Millie didn't mention that," he said.

"I don't usually apprise Millie of my itinerary and if I did, she wouldn't tell you because it would be none of your business." I dumped the fliers in the bin and headed for the door.

He followed me, holding the door open as I swept out into the street. "I think you're bluffing. Tell me what you're up to."

I stopped on the sidewalk and looked back at him, using my most innocent expression. "Honestly, Mike, I have no idea what you're talking about."

Mew! Meow!

Nero and Marlowe appeared at my feet. How did they get into town so fast? They ran over to Mike, circling around his ankles and purring. He bent down to pet them.

"Josie, I don't mean to be nosy, but this could be dangerous." He stood, towering over me, which is no easy task because I'm five-foot-seven. "I just don't want you to get hurt."

Meroo!

Apparently Nero agreed with him.

"Don't worry about me. I can take care of myself." I turned to walk toward my car, but he latched onto my elbow, holding it gently but swinging me around to face him. My arm tingled, my heart fluttered, but my brain got annoyed with his insistence.

"Josie, I think I know who the killer is. I was with Internal Affairs in the navy and have experience with this sort of thing. Leave it to me." His face showed only concern, not ego or pushiness, but I wasn't going to leave it to him. For one, I doubted he was going to nail his old high-school sweetheart and for two it was important for me to prove that I could do this. Plus, I had it all planned out with the Weatherbys, and what could possibly go wrong?

I extracted my elbow gently. "I think I know who it is too and the wheels are already set in motion. And besides, I'm not stupid and I'm not a kid anymore. I think I can solve this without your help."

Chapter Twenty-One

Despite the confidence I'd had about catching the killer when I'd talked to Mike outside the post office, I was jittery as a chihuahua in winter. I was half afraid he'd stick around the guesthouse, as I knew he suspected I was up to something. But he must have believed my story about going away. He finished up work and bid me farewell at four, asking about my flight. I told him I was taking a train, just in case he had designs on checking up on me at the airport. I had a twinge of guilt as I watched him drive off. He'd acted a little cool all afternoon and I hoped I hadn't been too harsh with him outside the post office.

At 6:30 p.m. Ron and Iona got the ball rolling by ushering everyone to the Marinara Mariner. Their plan was to get seated with all the others, then Ron would excuse himself to go to the bathroom and double back. He wanted to be here to make the arrest.

We figured the killer would come in the front door and head straight down the hall to the west wing. They wouldn't try the window for fear it would be locked, and why bother when they knew the front door would be unlocked and no one home? I turned off the lights and Ron and I crouched in the pitch-black doorway to the butler's pantry and waited.

At around 7:15 we heard a noise. Only problem was, it wasn't at the front door.

"That sounds like the kitchen," I whispered to Ron.

"Why would someone come in the kitchen?" Ron whispered back.

"I have no idea."

Mom and Millie knew about the plan so they wouldn't be coming in that door. Flora had already left for the day and she never came back to the guesthouse after work. Could it be Mike? I knew he'd seen through my act at the post office but surely he wouldn't ruin our plan.

Ron stood and the floor creaked.

"Shhh..."

We froze, but the creak must not have bothered the intruder because the next thing we heard was the squeak of the hinges as the kitchen door opened. Good thing I hadn't oiled them.

Ron tapped my arm and pointed to the kitchen, communicating that we should sneak over there quietly—it wasn't as if I couldn't have figured that one out on my own. One end of the butler's pantry opened into the kitchen and we tiptoed through. The kitchen was dark, but I could make out a form bending over the counter. By the size, shape and cloying smell of floral-scented perfume wafting over, I could tell it was Stella.

It *had* been her all along! But why was she standing at the kitchen counter? It looked like she was going through the recipes. Had she hidden something in the recipe box or cookbook? Could it be the rest of the note they'd found in Charles's room? Or maybe she wanted to swipe a recipe before heading into the west wing to look for the fake evidence I'd found. Either way she wasn't going to complete her mission.

I flicked on the light switch and jumped into the room. "Aha!"

"We caught you red-handed!" Ron chimed in.

Stella whirled around, squinting into the light. Her hands flew out, palms up in front of her. She dropped the paper she was holding and it floated down to the floor.

"What is that?" I pointed to the paper. "Part of the note Charles left?"

"A confession maybe," Ron said. Did he have to add something every time I spoke?

"Hardly." Stella put her hands down and glared at us.

"Fine." Ron whipped out his badge, the gold shield glinting in the light as he thrust it out toward her. "I'll be calling the police then and they'll get a confession from you."

"For what?" Stella crossed her arms over her chest. "I hardly think the police will care that I came to borrow a recipe."

I glanced at the floor. Yep. Looked like a recipe.

"Not for that," Ron said. "For poisoning gulls and killing Charles Prescott."

"What? I never killed anyone! Or poisoned anyone for that matter. Except that time Mr. Dudley got sick from my cream puffs but that was unintentional."

"Of course you killed Charles. He found out you were poisoning the gulls and threatened to blackmail you, so you had to kill him," I said.

Mew.

That sounded like Nero out in the parlor. Not sure what he was meowing about but apparently he hadn't figured out that all the action was going on here in the kitchen.

Stella made a face. "I'm not poisoning the gulls. Who told you that?"

"No one told me. It's as plain as day that they are affecting your business." I gestured in the direction of her inn.

Meow.

Was that Marlowe? It sounded like she was near the front stairway.

"They are not. I admit it's hard to keep up with cleaning the gull poop off the deck, but tourists love to go and feed the gulls. In fact, I have special 'gull food' canisters now that I sell them specifically for feeding the birds." Stella shrugged at our disbelieving looks. "It's just stale bread but hey, if life gives you lemons you make lemonade."

I glanced at Ron. He was stroking his chin and studying Stella. "Then why did you break in here tonight if not to get the evidence before it was given to the police?"

Stella sighed and pointed at the scrap of paper on the floor. "Okay, I admit it. I wasn't borrowing a recipe. I was returning one."

"Returning?" I bent down to pick up the paper.

"Yes. It's Millie's sour-cream-coffee-cake recipe. It's really delicious, so I stole it to make for the cooking contest. I wanted to sneak in and return it sooner, but after you came over and started asking all the questions about why I was hanging around the guesthouse, I didn't dare. So when I heard you wouldn't be here and the place would be unlocked, I figured it was a perfect time to return it."

I stared at the paper in my hand. Handwritten on a blue-lined index card and smudged with an old butter stain was Millie's distinctive handwriting in faded ink. It was the missing sour-cream-coffee-cake recipe. Had Stella really broken in just to return it or was this some clever trick to use as an excuse to be here because she really was breaking in to get the trumped-up evidence?

"But it has to be you," I said.

Meroo!

That one came from the hallway; probably the cats were figuring out we had the killer cornered in the kitchen. But now, looking at the recipe, I had to wonder if we'd made a mistake.

"Why does it have to be me? I'm not the only one who could poison the gulls. Why don't you ask Barbara Littlefield? She's the one who was conspiring with Charles up on the cliff."

Now I knew she was lying. "But Barbara said she never met Charles and she—"

A gruff voice in the doorway cut off my words. "That's right. I said what I had to say to stop you from nosing around."

We turned in the direction of the voice to see Barbara Littlefield standing in the doorway with a gun pointed directly at us.

Chapter Twenty-Two

I'd been so focused on getting Stella to confess that I didn't hear Barbara coming in.

Meow!

Nero and Marlowe appeared behind her, blinking at me as if I was the dumbest human on earth. I guess that's what they'd been meowing about. They'd been trying to warn me.

"Aren't you the building inspector?" Ron asked.

"Yeah, what of it?" Barbara glared at him.

"What do you have to do with all this?" Ron looked genuinely perplexed and for good reason. Why would Barbara kill Charles? Was she the one poisoning the gulls? Even Stella seemed confused as she glanced from the small silver gun Barbara was waving around to Ron to me.

"Did you know Charles from before?" I asked. Maybe she had a grudge. Maybe she'd been one of the many he'd had an affair with and was out for revenge.

"No. That dimwit thought he could outsmart me, though. Ha!" Barbara jerked the gun toward the door to the basement. "Now all three of you shuffle over toward the cellar nice and slow."

I glanced at the door and shivered. I'd only been down in the basement once and that was plenty for me.

It was an old house and the basement was dark, dank, and full of spiders the size of kittens.

Meow.

Nero rubbed up against Barbara's ankle.

She shook her foot to push him away.

"Get lost, kitty." Her face twisted even more. "I thought I told you not to have cats in the kitchen. It's a code violation. I'd write you up, but after I burn the place you won't even have a kitchen."

"But why would Charles blackmail you?" Ron asked.

Barbara gestured with the gun again and we all shuffled a bit closer to the door. "He shouldn't have been up on the cliff. I mean, what kind of a stupid cookbook uses flockenberries? They don't taste that good, you know."

"The gulls seem to like them," Stella said.

"Yeah. Unfortunately. That's how he found out." Barbara gestured with the gun again and we moved another half inch.

Meow!

Marlowe scratched Barbara's ankle. Barbara lashed out with her foot. Luckily, she missed the cat. Unluckily she kept her grip on the gun and her eyes on us. I had to wonder if the cats were trying to distract her.

"Found out about what?" I prompted. Maybe if she got talkative there'd be enough time for one of the others to come back and save us.

A sly look came over Barbara's face. "About what I was doing to the flockenberries. Someone had to get rid of those nuisance berry plants. Still hadn't perfected the poison, though; I had a few experiments going on."

I remembered the dead plants in her office. Had she been experimenting on those?

"So you poisoned the berries to get rid of the gulls?" Ron asked.

"No. Not the gulls, but hey, they *are* a nuisance. Town should thank me. I was trying to save the louse-wort from getting choked out. If the lousewort dies, the cliff will no longer be protected and next thing you know a big giant hotel will be looming over us ruining the quaint ambiance of the town."

"That's preposterous," Ron said. "Those lousewort plants must have been there for generations."

Merooo!

Marlowe wound around Barbara's feet and she glanced down annoyed but then looked right back up at us. Guess she didn't want to be distracted too long for fear one of us would lunge for the gun, which, of course, had been exactly my plan.

"That's where you're wrong. That lousewort was never here. I imported it and planted it to stop the hotel from being built. Cost me a pretty penny and was a lot of work keeping it thriving. And you people," Barbara waved the gun at me and Stella and we jumped back, "don't even appreciate my efforts! Now where would the town be if I hadn't done that!"

I remembered Jen had mentioned that Barbara got dirty packages. Had it been the lousewort? Where had she imported it from? I knew it was protected here in New England, but thought I'd heard my mother mention something about it growing like a weed in some other country. Maybe she'd sent away for it. No wonder she'd had to spend so much time "mothering" it if it hadn't naturally sprouted on the cliff.

But none of that mattered now. The only thing that did was making sure we did not get forced down into that basement.

Barbara smiled, but it wasn't a warm and fuzzy smile, it was cold and calculating mixed with a bit of pride. She shoved the gun forward. "To the basement door!"

We shuffled over more. Now we were right next to the door. Time was running out. I glanced at my watch.

Barbara laughed. "Hoping someone will come back early from dinner? Hardly. It's only eight o'clock and your guests will be at the Marinara Mariner for another hour at least. Guess your little plan to lure the killer here didn't work out so well after all."

"Well, it did lure the killer here…" Even facing death, I felt defensive of my plan.

"Yeah, but it gave me an even better idea. Now that I have to get rid of you and the evidence, a nice fire will do the trick!"

My gut clenched. She was planning to shove us in the basement and set the place on fire. My mind raced. I had to do something to stop her. I glanced around for a weapon, but only saw bowls, dish towels, and canisters.

Barbara moved forward, stepping on Nero's tail and earning a screech and hiss from him. "Open the basement door and shove those cats down there first."

Nero looked up at Barbara and wrinkled his nose, then glanced at me. My heart clenched at the thought of the cats burning in a fire. At least maybe I could save them.

"Not the cats. Let them go, they're innocent."

"Yeah," Stella agreed. "Killing us is one thing but not innocent kitties."

I glanced at Stella. She actually had a heart.

If the cats could understand Barbara, they were being awfully calm about their fate. Marlowe stretched and Nero trotted over to the cellar door. He glanced up at me and then at the doorknob. Suddenly I got an idea.

"OK. I see we have no choice but to go down there. Stand back, though. The door sticks and I need some room." Stella and Ron stood back and I grabbed the knob.

The cats sat to attention, eyes on Barbara, tails swishing on the floor.

I planted my feet and tugged. I twisted the knob. I made a show of trying to open the door, holding my breath and letting my face turn red. I glanced at Barbara. "It won't open."

Barbara rolled her eyes. "Figures. This old place isn't even worth fixing up. Good thing I wrote all those violations. I'm doing the town a favor by burning it down." She stomped over to the door. "Let me try. You're wimpy."

But just as she reached me, I whipped the door open. The movement surprised her and she teetered at the opening. Marlowe and Nero sprang into action, weaving around her feet. I gave her one hard shove.

She stumbled forward, tripping over the cats and losing her grip on the gun. It clattered to the floor.

And then, as she was teetering at the top of the stairs, Stella gave her one last push and she fell down into the dark hole of the basement.

"I'll get you for this!" Her words were punctuated by "Ouch!" and "Dang!" as she hit each stair going down.

Ron dove for the gun and I slammed the door shut just as the kitchen door burst open and Mike and Sheriff Chamberlain ran in.

They skidded to a stop, taking in the three of us standing there and the two cats planted firmly in front of the door, calmly licking their paws and washing behind their ears as a fresh string of curses drifted up from the basement.

Sherrif Chamberlain's eyes were wide, his gun held straight out in front of him. He glanced at Mike. "Well? Which one of them is the killer?"

*

Seth Chamberlain hauled Barbara out of the cellar, slapped the cuffs on her, and shoved her in the squad car with the energy of an eager rookie. We were standing in the driveway, the cats preening around us as if they'd been the ones to capture the killer. Inside the car, Barbara pounded on the window.

"You let me out of here, Seth Chamberlain. I've done a lot for this town and don't you forget it!"

We moved away from the car so we couldn't hear her.

"Sorry for acting like I suspected you, Josie," Seth said as he fished some cat treats out of his pocket and flipped them to Nero and Marlowe.

"What do you mean *acting*?" I asked.

Seth smiled and for a second I could see what Millie saw in him. Even though he had to be in his late seventies, the dimpled smile and intelligent twinkle in his eye gave him a boyish charm. "Heck, I knew it wasn't you all along. That was just an act. I would have arrested you if I had really thought it was you, seeing as there was evidence pointing in your direction. I didn't want the real killer to know I was on to them until I got solid evidence." He glanced uneasily at Ron and Stella.

I sensed that Seth was telling the truth about not suspecting me, but I doubted he'd known who the real killer was. More likely he'd suspected Ron or Stella just as I had. After all, he had asked Mike which one the killer was when they came bursting in. At least he'd ruled me out early on.

Speaking of Mike, he'd been fussing around me ever since they'd arrived and I wished he'd stop.

"I knew you were up to something when I ran into you in the post office," he said. "I figured you were luring the killer in with that trumped-up story and it was a good ploy. I just wish I'd gotten here sooner. It took me a while to explain it to Seth and get him moving."

"My gut instincts were spot on, but I didn't think anyone would believe me so I had to do something to flush the killer out." I didn't mention I had actually thought it was Stella.

He stepped closer and tucked a stray piece of hair behind my ear. Stella scowled at us.

"You could have been hurt. I wouldn't have liked that very much," he said softly.

Yeah, me either. "Why not?"

"Well, for one your brother would kill me and for two…" He hesitated then shoved his hands in his pockets and stepped back. "I'm kind of getting used to you being back in town."

"Thanks." For once I was at a loss for words. I felt like something had happened between us. Not sure what, but it wasn't entirely unwelcome. It was just too soon. For a second I regretted hiring Ed O'Hara to do the rest of the renovations so I wouldn't have to keep Mike on. I was going to miss having Mike at the guesthouse. It was probably for the best, though; I still needed to prove that I could be good on my own before I was ready to add another person to the mix. Plus, Ed charged a lot less.

Millie's 1970s Dodge Dart careened into the driveway and Mom and Millie spilled out, cell phones in hand.

"Did we miss it?" Millie asked.

"The police scanner app never went off!" Mom scowled at her phone.

Seth walked over and gave them a stern look. "We didn't put in a call this time. Now you ladies can't be using some app to go to all the crime scenes. It's dangerous."

Millie drew herself to her full height. "Why, Seth Chamberlain, you know darn well that without us, most of the crimes in this town would go unsolved. Besides, the crime scenes are not dangerous because the crime has already been committed."

"That's right," Mom chimed in. "And crime scenes are swarming with police, therefore very safe."

Seth closed his eyes and I imagined that he was mentally counting to ten. I couldn't blame him, I'd had to do that myself a few times when dealing with Mom and Millie.

He smiled at Millie. "It's true that you help immensely, but I would appreciate it if you don't broadcast that all over town. I have a reputation to protect."

Mom and Millie looked contrite. "Of course, sorry." Millie patted his arm. "There will be an extra dozen chocolate-chip cookies for you this weekend."

Seth's smile widened and he covered her hand with his. Millie grinned up at him, batted her eyes a few times and then slid her hand out from under his and tore away.

"I'm glad you understand, but now we have to go get the scoop from Josie!"

They scurried to my side. Mike was still standing there and Mom beamed at him. "I see you're watching out for my girl."

Mike smiled. "Can't let anything happen to her."

I bristled. "I'm a grown woman and don't need anyone to watch over me."

"Never mind that," Millie said. "Tell us all about it! How did the killer end up being Barbara? I thought it was Stella!"

By the time I was done telling them what had happened, the other guests were pulling into the driveway. Iona rushed to Ron to get the lowdown from him, and they beckoned Tina to join them, which she did reluctantly.

Mike had drifted off and was chatting with Stella. I didn't really mind—I mean, he was free to talk to whoever he wanted, but for some annoying reason I kept glancing in their direction as if I cared. A few times I caught Mike's eye. He had a smug expression every time he caught me looking, which I ignored.

Ava strode over to us, nodding her head as if she'd known what was unfolding the whole time. "Well, things sure are interesting at the Oyster Cove Guesthouse."

"Never a dull moment," Millie said.

"I knew something was going on," Ava said. "It's good to know my reporter's instincts are still working. Too bad people don't give a monkey's banana about society happenings anymore. It's OK, though, I have something better in mind."

Ava walked off with a satisfied look on her face and I got a little worried.

"I hope she's not going to write some sensational newspaper article about this," I said to Millie.

Millie's brows drew together. "Me too. Then again, maybe it would bring in business. You know how morbid people are."

"Hmm...you have a point."

"Never mind that." Mom tugged on my arm. "Mike's leaving. You're not going to let him get away, are you?"

I glanced over at his car, half expecting to see Stella inside, but she wasn't. "Yes, I think I am."

"Are you sure? Could be your last chance to get him to ask you out on a date," Mom said. "Millie said he finished up the last task on his list today."

"I'm not in the market for a date," I said. "Besides, it's probably for the best if he doesn't hang around here too much. The way he calls me 'Sunshine' is annoying."

As I watched his truck turn onto the road, I felt a little tug of regret. Now that he wouldn't be working at the guesthouse, I probably wouldn't see him much, but surely that was for the best.

Meow!

Meroo!

Nero and Marlowe joined our circle and Millie and Mom bent down to scratch their ears. The two cats strutted around, tails in the air and heads held high.

"Sheesh, by the way they're acting, you'd think they'd caught the killer," Mom said.

"They sure do look proud of something." Millie glanced up at me, her brows raised in a question.

I looked down at the two cats. They met my gaze with intelligent, luminescent eyes. "Funny you say that. I think they did actually help out. It was due to them getting underfoot that we were able to push Barbara into the basement."

Millie looked adoringly at the cats, a proud smile on her face. "I say, they are certainly taking good care of the guesthouse and their new human. What do you say, Josie?"

"I agree. In fact I'm getting used to their company. I can't imagine the guesthouse without them."

Meow!

Meress!

Chapter Twenty-Three

"I'm so proud that you caught a killer all by yourself while running a new business, Mom." Emma's voice gushed over the phone, swelling my heart with pride. "But it sounds like that could have been dangerous."

"Not at all. Sheriff Chamberlain was right outside the door." I made it sound like I'd arranged for the sheriff to step in so Emma would think I was never in danger.

"Even so, I don't know what I'd do if anything happened to you," she said.

"You don't need to worry about me. I'm sure nothing like that will happen again. I mean, what are the odds?"

Emma laughed. "Good point. I gotta run. You take care. Love you, Mom."

"Love you too." I barely got the words out before she disconnected. Kids these days, always running off. Truth was, I'd wanted to give her the same heartfelt warning about her job at the FBI. I took some comfort in the fact that she was an analyst and not in the field, but still, a mother never stops worrying. Unless maybe you were talking about *my* mother. She seemed to thrive on danger and it didn't seem to matter which one of us was in it.

It was one week after Barbara's arrest and Millie, Mom, and I sat in the kitchen at the Oyster Cove Guesthouse. Steam wafted up from mugs of coffee that sat beside warm pieces of sugary sour-cream coffee cake on the table in front of us. Nero and Marlowe were there too, of course. They'd been treated like royalty all week and were now lapping up the last of a small bit of cream I'd given them as a treat.

"At least Stella Dumont did the right thing and decided not to use my coffee-cake recipe for the contest." Millie forked up a piece of the crumbly top.

"That would have been cheating," my mother said. "What's she using instead?"

"Her Aunt Sally's fruitcake, I think," Millie said.

Mom laughed. "I doubt that will win any prizes."

I relaxed back in my chair. Honestly, I hadn't been worried about Stella winning that contest and getting one up on me anyway. Not much. I was sure my baking would improve over time. Besides, considering how often Millie popped in to help make the breakfasts, I was sure the Oyster Cove Guesthouse would be able to keep its reputation for good eats.

"It's nice not to have guests to tend to."

Ava had left two days earlier for a cruise to the Caribbean. The Weatherbys had gone off on a top-secret mission to Antarctica the day after Barbara was arrested, and Tina had broken off her affair with Tony and gone back home on Tuesday. I was glad their affair was over; I liked the chicken parmesan at the Marinara Mariner and didn't want the restaurant to close down if Tony and the Mrs. got divorced.

"I think things went very well for your first round of guests." Millie pressed her index finger to the plate to pick up the last sweet crumbs from the coffee cake, licked them off and then pushed up from the table and headed to the cabinets where she started to assemble bowls, whisks, and measuring utensils. Apparently she was going to do some baking. I knew the kitchens were small over at the retirement village, but honestly, if she was going to just keep coming here to bake she might as well make the breakfasts all the time.

At my skeptical look, my mother added, "Well, there was that little hiccup of a murder, but you handled it very well, dear." Mom patted my arm.

"And caught the killer!" Millie added.

Meow!

Meroo?

"Yes, we know you guys helped too," Millie said to Nero and Marlowe, who appeared offended at the lack of credit. They twitched their whiskers and sauntered off toward the hallway, apparently appeased by Millie's praise.

"Who would have figured it was Barbara?" Mom said. "I mean, I knew she went overboard tending to the lousewort but I never thought she'd planted it herself. I would have suspected Ava before Barbara, but I was hoping it was Stella."

"Me too," I said.

Millie turned around to look at us. "Ava? Why would you suspect her?"

"She knew Charles from before, she was the one who told us about Tina, she was here at the guesthouse . . . it sort of seemed like she turned up everywhere," I said. "I just hope she isn't going to do some big column in the paper about it. It sounded like she needed something exciting to bring in readers."

"Don't worry, she isn't writing a column." Millie glanced out into the hallway to make sure we couldn't be overheard. By whom I had no idea as we were the only ones in the guesthouse. "She's writing a book about it."

"Oh." Was that better than a column? Probably. Maybe they'd make it into a movie and people would flock here to see where it happened.

"I'm just glad all's well that ends well," Mom said. "Barbara would have done anything to protect herself, so it's a good thing you guys were able to outwit her."

"I can't believe she would have burned down the guesthouse." Millie shuddered as she cracked eggs into a bowl.

"Yeah that could have been a problem, especially with the town's two hundred and fiftieth celebration and all the descendants of Jedediah Biddeford coming to stay here in two weeks."

Though the guesthouse had been added to over the years, it had started out as a smaller mansion way before Millie's people even owned it. The main part of the mansion that was now the west wing had been origi- nally built by Jedediah Biddeford, and seeing as he'd lived here two hundred and fifty years ago, his descen- dants felt the town celebration was a great time to have a family reunion right in the house that started it all.

A family reunion was nice, but I was really thrilled

because all five of the rooms that had been renovated to this point had been booked by Biddefords. If only I'd kept Mike on, I might have been able to squeak out a few more rooms, but it was just as well that he wouldn't be around. I was getting too comfortable with him. And while Ed O'Hara was a bit slow, he did good work and I was happy to supplement his Social Security income.

"They're probably only coming because of the curse," Millie said as she whisked something together in a stainless-steel bowl.

"Curse?" The familiar baritone came from the doorway. I hoped I was hearing things. I scrunched my eyes shut and turned in that direction, opening one eye slowly. Mike Sullivan lounged against the doorframe. Who had invited *him*? To be even more annoying, he winked at me. "Hey, Sunshine, how's our little detective?"

"I thought you were done with your work here," I said.

"I am." Mike pushed off the frame and strode over to Millie, kissing her on the cheek. "Aunt Millie invited me over for cookies."

"I'm just getting ready to put them in the oven now." She scooped big dollops of batter out of the bowl with a tablespoon and plunked them on a cookie sheet.

"Forget about the cookies, what's this about a curse?" Mom asked.

Millie waved her hand in the air dismissively, keeping her back to us as she continued dropping cookie dough onto the sheets. "Oh, just some old curse where

Jedediah claimed he was coming back at the town's two hundred and fiftieth to deal with anyone who dared plunder his treasure."

"Treasure?" Mom's eyes lit up like a slot machine on tilt. "I never heard anything about a treasure."

Millie opened the oven and shoved the cookie sheets in. "My grandmother told me about it when I was a little girl. Apparently, it was told to her grandfather when they bought the place. But there's no treasure. Jedediah was sailing to the West Indies and figured he'd come back with treasure, but he never made it back to the country."

"Why not?" Mike asked.

Millie shrugged. "How should I know? Died over there. Plague or something."

"So why have a curse then?" I asked.

"Sounds like he was overly dramatic. Probably setting the stage, getting everyone scared for when he did bring back the treasure so no one dared mess with it. You know how superstitious people were back then." Millie put the dirty dishes in the sink and started running the water.

Merooo!

The cats' hollow cry came from deep inside the mansion. It was kind of eerie and reminded me of the way they'd sounded the morning we'd found Charles Prescott's body. Must be a strange echo coming from that room…

"But there could still be a treasure," Mom said hopefully. I could already tell she was dreaming of treasure maps and X-marks-the-spot. Probably already planning her trip to Ace Hardware to buy a shovel.

Millie turned around, her hands on her hips. "Really, Rose. If there were a treasure don't you think someone would have found it by now?"

Mom looked disappointed. "I suppose."

Mereech!

This time everyone looked in the direction of the cry.

"Is that Marlowe?" Millie cocked her head to the side. "I hope she's not hurt."

"I'll go see," Mike said.

"Me too." If something was going on in the guesthouse, I certainly didn't want Mike one-upping me like he'd tried to do with the Prescott investigation.

I followed Mike into the hall to the sounds of another loud cry from the cats.

"Sounds like it's coming from the west wing near where we found Charles Prescott," Mike said.

"Lucky thing there can't be another dead body in there now, no one else is in the guesthouse." I didn't feel as confident about that as I sounded.

Mike scowled as he tried to open the door that separated the main house from the west wing. "It's locked. That's good. You're supposed to keep it shut, especially if you have new guests staying here."

Okay, now I remembered why I had hired Ed in his place. Mike was kind of bossy. I didn't need that. "Yeah, I know. You sound like Barbara."

I ducked into the pantry and retrieved the ring with the spare sets of keys to unlock the various doors that didn't go to the guests' rooms. I kept the keys to the guests' rooms in a more secure place.

Meroow!

Mike frowned at the keys jangling in my hand. "Are those keys easily accessible to anyone?".

I paused before opening the door, my annoyance with Mike overshadowing my worry about the cats. "What's it to you?"

He smiled, a twinkle in his eye that I did not like. "Oh, it's very important to me."

What was that supposed to mean?

Meoooo!

"That sounds bad." Mike's face creased with worry. "We better get in there."

I pushed the door open, my stomach tightening as I glanced over at the stairs. No dead body. I felt silly. Of course there wouldn't be one.

Meroop.

The sound came from the next room.

"I think they're over here."

Mike headed toward the sound. I gave one last glance at the place where Charles had been found. Ed had started to work on this part of the guesthouse and the fallen banister and wooden debris had been cleaned up. There was no sign that a man had died there just over a week ago. Good, I was glad to put that whole incident behind me.

Meroeeow!

Never mind that the cats' cries sounded eerily similar to the tone and insistency they'd had when they'd alerted me to Charles's body. I was more worried about what Mike had just said. Why would anything at the guesthouse be important to him? If he thought he was going to make it a habit to pop over all the time I'd have to set him straight.

I followed him to the room. Millie had said that it had once been a small ballroom. Remnants of black-and-white marble tile dotted the floor, water-stained floral wallpaper peeled from the walls, and the ceiling still had chunks of plaster medallions that once surrounded grand chandeliers. I wasn't going to restore it to a ballroom, as there was little interest in balls these days. My plan was to make it into a game room. Judging by the clouds of dust in the air, the cobwebs in the corners and the smell of decades' old dry wood, that was going to take a lot of work.

Mew!

Nero and Marlowe were at the far wall. Thankfully they seemed unharmed and I wondered if all the incessant meowing was simply because they were admiring themselves in the few shards left of the full-length mirror that still clung to the wall. Right now it reflected the dilapidated room, but I imagined guests in ball gowns and elbow-length gloves waltzing around on the dance floor, their images reflected in the gigantic mirror, making the room look twice as large and the crowd twice as big.

"This place is in bad shape." Mike stood in the middle of the room surveying its entirety. I doubted he was picturing ballroom dancers. He might have been picturing a ball, but it was probably more like a wrecking ball.

Meow! Nero's cry was insistent, as if we weren't paying enough attention.

"It looks like they're fine," I said. Though I didn't like the way Marlowe was scratching at the wall and then looking back at me. It was almost the same way she'd looked at me when we'd discovered Charles. But that was crazy, there was clearly no dead body in this room.

"You'll need to make sure you shore up these joists before you do any work here. This room is big and that's a load-bearing wall over there. You'll want to submit plans and get the proper inspections before you mess around with it," Mike said.

Now he was really starting to bug me. "I think I can handle it and Ed knows what he's doing. Besides, the renovations here aren't your business anymore and I sincerely doubt you'll be coming around much anyway, right?" Maybe I sounded a little too hopeful with that last part because Mike's eyes darkened with disappointment for a second before returning to their devilish twinkle.

"Sorry, Sunshine, that's where you're wrong."

Somehow those six little words were more disturbing than the prospect of the cats finding another dead body inside the guesthouse.

"What do you mean?" I asked cautiously.

Mike's smile widened. "Haven't you heard? What goes on here is going to be very much my business from here on out. I'm taking over as building inspector, at least until they find someone else to take Barbara's place. So, you see, I'll be coming around here a lot more—especially considering all the work you have going on and the decrepit state of this part of the mansion. Why, you might even see me more than you did when I worked here."

Nero's despairing cry echoed my thoughts. I gaped at Mike, remembering how Barbara would just waltz in unannounced all the time. Was he planning to do the same?

But Mike was no longer paying attention to me. He was over near the cats, bent down petting them. They butted their furry heads against his hand and purred. Clearly *they* wouldn't mind him coming around all the time. Traitors.

"What have you got here?" Mike bent closer to the wall where the cats had been pawing and scratching. He poked at it with his finger, sniffed, then looked up at me. "Looks like you might have a problem with rot here, maybe even mold."

Perfect. "I'm sure Ed will address it when he gets to this part. Don't worry, I'll make sure we follow proper inspection procedures."

Meow! Nero clawed at the wall.

Meroo! Marlowe butted her head against it.

"Yes, I heard him, Marlowe. The wall needs attention. Don't worry, I'll see to it that everything gets fixed properly." I didn't relish the idea of Mike hanging around inspecting all the renovations, but I was glad that the cats weren't hurt and all they were crying about was some rotted boards. After all, I'd dealt with a dead body here at the guesthouse, how hard could it be to tackle a little bit of rot and mold?

*

Nero rolled his eyes and scratched at the wall again. Josie just wasn't getting it. And here he'd thought she was starting to clue in to their attempts at communication.

"I don't think she's on the same page as us," Marlowe purred as Mike scratched the top of her head.

"No kidding. She's no Millie, that's for sure." Nero's whiskers twitched and he held back a sneeze. The moldy smell emitting from the wall was ten times stronger than it was to the humans due to his highly developed senses. And he was incredibly allergic to mold. But the mold and rot weren't the only scents coming from the wall, not that Josie was noticing. She was too busy pretending to act nonchalant around Mike.

"Ahh, Millie. I wish she hadn't left the guesthouse to us. It's such a huge responsibility." Marlowe licked her paw and pushed it behind her ear. "But at least we redeemed ourselves for not preventing Charles Prescott's murder." Marlowe glanced at Nero out of the corner of her eye hopefully.

"Indeed. I do think we did. We led Josie to many of the clues and if not for our fancy footwork Barbara might not have been safely dispatched into the cellar where she could do no harm."

"Not that we got a lot of credit for either of those things." Marlowe stretched against the wall, running her front claws down it, creating an annoying sound.

"Ahh, but that is for the best. Their fragile egos couldn't take it if they knew most of the detecting was done by us and our feline friends." Nero glanced up at Josie. She wasn't paying the least bit of attention to them or to the wall or the scratches Marlowe had just made in the remnants of wallpaper left on it. She was busy scowling at Mike. Judging by the snatches of conversation, they were arguing about how often Mike, as the building inspector, could come by unannounced. Nero didn't see what the problem was. Mike gave good belly rubs and always treated the cats kindly. Maybe Josie should let him give her a belly rub and she'd be more accommodating to his visits?

"I suppose you are right. They are a strange breed, but we need to keep them happy. Otherwise who will buy the treats and gravy-laden cat food from the store for us?" Marlowe said.

"Exactly. Make them think they are the brains of the operation." Nero smiled at the younger cat. She was coming along splendidly and Nero was pleased with the way she'd caught on to some of the clues in the investigation. It would be a long time before she was as good as Nero himself was, but she was showing promise. At least Marlowe was trainable. Josie on the other hand…well, Nero was a little worried about whether or not she would ever come up to speed.

The two humans left the room, still arguing, and Nero waited a few beats so they wouldn't think he was trotting after them obediently or anything—that type of behavior was for dogs.

"Well, we've done our best to alert Josie," Nero said after he heard the lock on the door click shut. It didn't bother him that they were locked into the west wing. He knew dozens of secret exits and entrances into many of the rooms in the mansion. "Let's go see if Millie is still in the kitchen and try to finagle some of those bacon-flavored cat treats while we contemplate how to better communicate with our resident human."

"Good idea." Marlowe trotted along after him. "But I hope Josie starts catching on a little quicker because, if she doesn't, she may be in for a big surprise when Ed really gets going on that room renovation."

A Letter from Leighann

Hi! I hope you enjoyed *A Twist in the Tail*. If you did enjoy it and want to keep up-to-date with all my latest releases, just sign up at the following link. Your email address will never be shared and you can unsubscribe at any time.

www.bookouture.com/leighann-dobbs

As an animal lover, I love putting pets in my books, especially cats. And as a cat owner…err, should I say cat servant…I find them fascinating and love imbuing the characters in my books with the traits of the many cats that have adopted me.

As a lifelong New Englander, I feel that there is no better setting for a book—especially the coast of Maine where this series is set. I also love writing about small towns, quirky characters, and intriguing mysteries.

I've combined all these to bring you the Oyster Cove Cozy Mystery Series. I hope you enjoy reading the books as much as I enjoyed writing them.

All best,
Lee

Join my email list to get all my latest releases at the lowest-possible price, plus, as a benefit for signing up today, I will send you a copy of a Leighann Dobbs book that hasn't been published anywhere...yet!

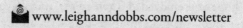 www.leighanndobbs.com/newsletter

If you are on Facebook, please join my VIP readers' group and get exclusive content and updates on all my books. It's a fun group where you can feel at home, ask questions, and talk about your favorite reads.

groups/ldobbsreaders

If you want to receive a text message on your cell phone when I have a new release, text COZYMYSTERY to 88202 (sorry, this only works for U.S. cell phones!).

@leighanndobbs

leighanndobbsbooks

www.leighanndobbs.com

Recipes

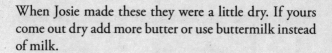

Lemon-Poppy Seed Muffins—Serves 12

When Josie made these they were a little dry. If yours come out dry add more butter or use buttermilk instead of milk.

Ingredients:
- ♥ 2 ½ cups all-purpose flour
- ♥ 1 ¾ teaspoons baking powder
- ♥ ¼ teaspoon baking soda
- ♥ ½ teaspoon salt
- ♥ ¾ cup granulated sugar
- ♥ ½ cup unsalted butter (1 stick), melted and cooled slightly
- ♥ ½ cup whole milk
- ♥ ½ cup sour cream
- ♥ 2 large eggs, room temperature
- ♥ 2 tablespoons fresh lemon juice
- ♥ 1 teaspoon lemon zest
- ♥ 4 teaspoons poppy seeds

Directions:
1. Heat oven to 350 degrees F or 177 degrees C.
2. Whisk the flour, baking powder, baking soda and salt together in a medium bowl.
3. Combine the sugar, butter, milk, eggs, sour cream, lemon juice, lemon zest and poppy seeds in a large bowl. Mix until well combined. Whatever you do, don't feed the cats lemon zest no matter how much they are begging for scraps. One sniff of that stuff and they go on a clawing rampage.

4. Fold the dry ingredients into the wet ingredients. Don't over-mix.

5. Divide the batter evenly between 12 muffin cups. Millie has the oldest muffin pan on the planet and uses paper liners. My ex used to use a silicone muffin pan and it's a lot easier to clean.

6. Bake for about 20 minutes. A toothpick inserted into the middle of a muffin should come out clean when they are ready. Let cool.

7. You could also whip up a glaze for these and it would be delicious. Josie is lucky if she can just get the muffins baked; maybe she will tackle glazing at some future date.

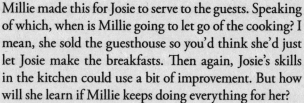

Broccoli Quiche—Serves 4

Millie made this for Josie to serve to the guests. Speaking of which, when is Millie going to let go of the cooking? I mean, she sold the guesthouse so you'd think she'd just let Josie make the breakfasts. Then again, Josie's skills in the kitchen could use a bit of improvement. But how will she learn if Millie keeps doing everything for her?

In the book, Millie made two pans of this, but this recipe from the author's mother's collection is for a serving of 4. They're big servings, though!

Ingredients:
- 3 eggs
- 3 oz. cheddar cheese, grated
- 10 oz. package of frozen broccoli, cooked and drained
- ⅛ teaspoon pepper
- 1 ½ cups hot cooked rice
- ¾ teaspoon salt
- 6 tablespoons skim milk

Directions:
1. Beat one egg. Add the rice, ½ the grated cheese and the salt. Mix well and press firmly in an even layer onto the bottom of an 8-inch pan.
2. Lightly beat the other two eggs. Stir in the broccoli, milk, pepper and the remaining cheese. Add this mixture to the pan.
3. Bake at 375 degrees F or 190 degrees C for 30 minutes.

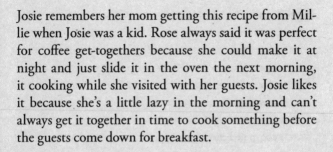

Brunch Egg Dish Casserole—Serves 8

Josie remembers her mom getting this recipe from Millie when Josie was a kid. Rose always said it was perfect for coffee get-togethers because she could make it at night and just slide it in the oven the next morning, it cooking while she visited with her guests. Josie likes it because she's a little lazy in the morning and can't always get it together in time to cook something before the guests come down for breakfast.

Ingredients:

- 7–10 slices of white bread, cubed
- 8 oz. cheddar cheese, shredded
- 8 eggs
- 3 cups skim milk
- ½ teaspoon salt
- ½ teaspoon pepper
- 1 teaspoon dry mustard
- 4 oz. ham, cubed

Directions:

1. Butter a 9 x 13-inch pan. Spread half the cubed bread on the bottom of the pan. Sprinkle half the cheese on top of the bread, then layer half the ham on top of that. Repeat these layers.

2. Beat eggs, milk, salt, pepper and mustard together. Pour on top of layered ingredients. Cover and refrigerate overnight.

3. The next morning, bake (covered) at 350 degrees F or 177 degrees C for 50–55 minutes.

Ham-and-Cheese Bisquick Puffs—Serves 12

Ingredients:
- 3 cups Bisquick
- 1 cup milk
- 2 eggs
- 3 tablespoons olive oil
- ¾ teaspoon salt
- ¾ cup ham, cubed
- ½ cup grated cheese (any type)

Directions:
1. Preheat oven to 400 degrees F or 200 degrees C.
2. Combine Bisquick, eggs, milk, olive oil and salt in a large bowl. Fold in the ham and grated cheese.
3. Pour batter evenly into 12 muffin cups (either silicone or with paper liners).
4. Bake for 20 minutes, until a toothpick inserted into muffin comes out clean.

Millie's Famous Sour-Cream Coffee Cake—Serves 10

Stella stole this recipe to enter in the contest, so Josie never got a chance to make it. But, since it was one of her favorites as a little girl, it's included here for you to try.

Ingredients:

- ½ cup salted butter
- ½ cup granulated sugar
- 1 large egg
- ½ cup sour cream
- ½ teaspoon vanilla extract
- 1 cup all-purpose flour
- ½ teaspoon baking powder
- ½ teaspoon baking soda
- ⅛ teaspoon salt

Topping:

- ¼ cup sugar
- ⅓ cup packed brown sugar
- 2 teaspoons ground cinnamon
- ½ cup chopped pecans

Directions:

1. Preheat oven to 350 degrees F or 190 degrees C.
2. Grease an 8 x 8-inch pan.
3. Combine the topping ingredients in a bowl and set aside.
4. In a large bowl, cream butter and sugar until fluffy. Add the egg and mix. Add the sour cream and vanilla. Mix well.

5. In a separate bowl mix the flour, baking soda, baking powder and salt.

6. Add the dry ingredients to the wet ingredients and mix until just combined.

7. Pour half the batter into the pan. Sprinkle half the topping mix over the batter. Spoon remaining batter on top. Sprinkle remaining topping mix on top of that.

8. Bake until a toothpick inserted in the middle comes out clean—about 40 minutes.

USA Today bestselling author Leighann Dobbs discovered her passion for writing after a twenty-year career as a software engineer. She lives in New Hampshire with her husband, Bruce, their trusty Chihuahua mix, Mojo, and beautiful rescue cat, Kitty. When she's not reading, gardening, making jewelry or selling antiques, she likes to write cozy mystery and historical romance books.

Learn more about Leighann Dobbs at:

leighanndobbs.com
Facebook.com/leighanndobbsbooks
Twitter @Leighanndobbs